D0008204

WITHDRAWN

ALSO BY LINDA CREW

Children of the River
Someday I'll Laugh About This

NEKOMAH CREEK

by Linda Crew

Illustrated by Charles Robinson

Delacorte Press
New York

Published by
Delacorte Press
Bantam Doubleday Dell Publishing Group, Inc.
666 Fifth Avenue
New York, New York 10103

Library of Congress Cataloging in Publication Data
Crew, Linda.
Nekomah Creek/by Linda Crew; illustrated by Charles Robinson.
p.   cm.
Summary: Nine-year-old Robby loves his noisy and somewhat unconventional
family, but unwanted attention from a counselor and a bully at school makes him
self-conscious about just how unconventional his family might look to outsiders.
ISBN 0-385-30442-0
[1. Family life—Fiction. 2. Schools—Fiction.] I. Robinson, Charles, 1931–   ill.
II. Title.
PZ7.C86815Ne   1991
[Fic]—dc20   90-49119   CIP   AC

Manufactured in the United States of America

November 1991

10 9 8 7 6 5 4 3 2 1

For my son Miles,
with love and special thanks
for the inspiration
of his own book, *Son of a Nut.*

CONTENTS

□ 1 □

Caught and Cornered

"So that's where you've been hiding!"

Mrs. Perkins's voice jerked me right out of my paperback and back to the real world.

"Robert Hummer." She pressed her lips together and frowned into the old dory where I'd been huddled down reading. "What am I going to do with you?"

A horrible gloom came over me. This peeling blue boat, beached in a pile of sand at the edge of the playground, had got me through a month of recesses. Why'd she have to come marching out here and find me now? I thought I was safe, what with the stretch of long wet grass between me and the merry-go-round. I should have known wet grass wouldn't bother old Mrs. Perkins in her thick-soled shoes.

Now when I say old, I don't really mean years. Mrs. Perkins was probably about average age for a grown-up. But something seemed old about her, like maybe she'd been thinking the exact same thoughts, over and over, for a real long time.

"Well, come on out now."

I climbed over the side and stood in front of her, clutching my well-worn copy of *Encyclopedia Brown #5.*

She put her hands on her hips. I won't say her *fat* hips. She was big but she was solid.

"Whatever is a healthy boy like you doing sitting here reading when you ought to be off playing with the other kids?"

I sighed. I'd already told her about five times—I hate recess.

Now I know that sounds weird. The other fourth graders all rip out like they've got rockets on their heels when that bell rings. Sixty seconds flat and they're lined up for tetherball or foursquare. But I'm not big on sports.

We'd been through all this before though, so why answer? She didn't want to hear it, just like she didn't want to hear how I wish she'd call me Robby, how I think the hokey pokey is totally dumb, how the story problems in math sometimes don't make any sense.

"If Johnny has fifty-five stamps," she'd read out loud this morning, "and he pastes five on each page, how many pages will he need?"

"But that's silly," I said, forgetting to raise my hand. "He could fit a lot more than five on each page. And besides, you don't *paste* stamps in the book. That wrecks them. You're supposed to use stamp hinges."

Mrs. Perkins just looked at the ceiling and took a deep breath like she was counting to keep calm. I guess extra talking loused up her schedule. Fifteen minutes for this, twenty minutes for that. She had to be totally organized.

"Robert," she said now, "I don't understand why you do this."

I shrugged, listening to the creek rushing by at the edge of the playing field. I wasn't the worst kid around by a long shot. I did my assignments. Unless you counted asking questions, I didn't goof off in class. So why'd Mrs. Perkins want to pick on me? Right now, over by the gym door, two eighth-grade girls were having a shouting match—trading names you wouldn't dare repeat to your mom and dad. Wouldn't you think Mrs. Perkins'd want to hustle over and break it up?

But no—she was too busy with me.

I sighed. "I just don't like sports."

"Oh, come now. All boys like sports."

Was I supposed to call her a liar or what? I stared at the grass. My shoes were getting soaked.

"This bookworm business is getting completely out of hand. I saw you trying to read during the film strip this morning. It's got to stop!"

She was right about that. Reading in the dark was hard on my eyes. I'd have to smuggle in the tiny flashlight I used under the covers at night.

She held out her hand. "Let's have the book, please."

I held it out. So long, Encyclopedia. I sighed. I'd been right in the middle of a case.

"Mrs. Perkins? Didn't you ever feel that what was happening in a book you were reading was more interesting than real life?"

She squinted at me like I was some weird bug in a box.

Well, gee. Seems to me lots of people like books or movies or television programs better than real life. When you've only got one life, in one place, it's fun to go off in your mind to other adventures.

And books are best, I think. TV only shows you the story—a book takes over your whole brain. It may look like nothing but paper, but open it and start reading and presto—you're in another world, maybe the past, maybe the future. It's like magic. Really. Think about it—characters made from little black markings coming alive, barging right into your head and carrying on their business there. Sometimes they never leave.

Mrs. Perkins ought to understand this. Every time she opened her desk drawer to put in my milk money I'd see a different paperback tucked in the corner—usually the kind where a lady in a swirly dress and too much hair is running away from a spooky castle . . .

She'd been looking off toward the creek. Now she turned back to me. "Why don't we go see what Mrs. Van Gent thinks about this."

I groaned. Not the new school counselor. What would Mom and Dad say? At the school board meeting, they'd stood up along with some of the other newer families and argued how important it was for Nekomah Creek School to have a counselor. But I figured they wanted a counselor to straighten out some of the wilder kids. I don't think they were picturing *me* getting dragged into her office.

"I hope she can fit you in," Mrs. Perkins said, hustling me toward the double doors at the primary side of the building. "If not it'll have to wait until *next* Monday."

Be busy, I prayed. *Please be too busy.* I glanced longingly at the third-grade classroom as we passed. Mrs. Kassel never seemed to think I was a problem last year. She used to laugh at my jokes. She thought it was great how I loved to read. She even had an old clawfoot bathtub full of pillows in her room just for flopping in with a book when you finished your other work.

Funny—with Mrs. Kassel it was like I couldn't do anything wrong, but with Mrs. Perkins I couldn't do anything right. Had I changed into a different kid over the summer or what?

Mrs. Perkins parked me in the hall and went into the little room next to the principal's office.

I'd never seen the counselor before. What would she be like?

After a couple of minutes this girl from my class came out. Amber Hixon. She wasn't crying, but her face had that pink-to-the-eyebrows, darned-if-I-will look.

She sniffed and stuck out her chin. "What are you doing here?" Her sandy-colored hair was one big cowlick in front, standing up straight and stubborn from her forehead, then flopping over.

"They're making me talk to the counselor," I said. "You too?"

She nodded. I could tell whatever happened in that room was no picnic.

"Pretty bad, huh?"

Amber crossed her arms over her chest and glared back at the door. "She comes on real nice, but you better watch what you say. That's my advice."

"What do you mean? What does she ask you?"

"About your family. Stuff that's none of her business. I'm not kidding, she's nothing but a big snoop. My mom's going to be sorry she ever gave them permission to talk to me."

"Why're they making you do it?"

She glowered. "It's so stupid. Stupid, stupid, stupid."

"What?"

"Oh, just 'cause of this picture I drew."

I didn't get it. Amber was a pretty good artist, and her pictures were always things like unicorns sailing over rainbows or princessy-looking girls picking flowers.

"It was just something I scribbled one day when I was mad at my mom and dad," Amber said. "I never meant anybody to see it. It musta fell out of my desk."

"Oh," I said, like this explained everything. "So it wasn't one of your unicorn pictures?"

"Ha. Not hardly."

Wow. What *had* she drawn? I was wondering if I dared ask when the door opened.

" 'Member, don't tell *nothing*," Amber whispered. Then she spun on her heel and marched off, hands knotted into fists.

Mrs. Perkins motioned me inside to a chair. She gave me one of those long, grown-up looks that you know are supposed to mean something, only you're not sure exactly what.

Then she sighed. "Mrs. Van Gent is here to help you, Robert. Please try to be honest with her."

"Okay." I hung my head. I thought I *was* always honest. I lifted my eyes. "Could I have my book back now?" I wanted something to hold on to.

"Why don't I just go ahead and return it to the library for you?"

"But it's my own."

She frowned at the book and checked the back

for a library card. That made me mad! I am not a liar!

"All the same," she said, "I believe I'll keep it at my desk for now. I don't want you peeking at it while Mrs. Van Gent's trying to talk to you."

My face got real hot. Guess she'd seen me pulling that in class.

She went out, leaving me to the counselor.

Mrs. Van Gent was a serious-looking woman wearing a gray suit and those high-heeled kind of shoes you see on TV but not very often around Nekomah Creek. She was really sort of pretty. You could tell she didn't care about that, though. She had big black glasses and blond hair twisted back into a tight bun. She was dressed for important business.

She rested her rear against the edge of the desk. "So, Robert . . ."

I looked up. "Could you call me Robby?"

"Oh, sure." She cleared her throat. "Robby. Why do you think your teacher wants you to talk to me?"

I squirmed. "Uh, because I read too much and I don't want to play with the other kids?" I watched to see if this was the right answer, but she wasn't saying. Her face looked friendly enough, though.

"Are you having trouble making friends?"

"No." I scratched my left shin with the heel of my right shoe. A nervous habit, my mom says. "I have friends."

"Why don't you want to play with them, then?"

I shrugged. I had more fun with my friends when they came to my house or I went to theirs. Then we could play Clue or build things with Construx or play spies in the woods. But playground stuff was all sports. Ben and Jason and the others had given up trying to get me in on it.

"I guess I'd just rather read," I said finally. "I get plenty of sports in PE."

"It's wonderful that you like to read so much. It's too bad we can't get more of the students interested in books the way you are."

Right, I thought. And then you could start bugging them about it too.

"Playing games outside is also important, though. We like everyone to be well-rounded."

Huh. Well-flattened was more like it. I thought about the last time I took a tetherball in the teeth.

The door connecting the room to the office opened and one of the secretaries handed Mrs. Van Gent a folder of papers. She sat down at the empty desk and studied them.

After a while she looked up. "You've had a big change at your house recently, haven't you, Robby?"

I thought. Then I nodded.

"Something that's been a bit hard on you?"

"Well, I didn't *like* it when my mom came home with her hair all frizzed like that, but it's *her* hair. I'll get used to it."

The counselor smiled. "No, Robby. I meant the twins."

"The twins? But we've had them for two years."

"Yes. Now I want you to be completely honest with me, Robby. How do you feel about your brother and sister?"

I shrugged. "I like 'em."

"Of course you do. But do you like *everything* about them?"

What was she getting at? Lucy and Freddie are the cutest babies in the whole world. I thought of the way they'd waved me off to school just that morning, standing on the porch railing. Dad held the backs of their Superman and Wonder Woman jammies so they wouldn't fall off while they jumped up and down, flapping all four arms, trying to outshout each other yelling "Bye! Bye! Bye! Bye! Bye!"

"Well, there *are* two things I don't like about 'em," I admitted. "Um . . . what they do in their diapers and spitting up."

"That's understandable."

I nodded, remembering the time I got carried away hugging Freddie—squeezed him to the popping point. He urped all over me. Yuck.

"Oh, and I hated having to give up going barefoot around the house."

"Why can't you go barefoot?"

I looked at her. "Have you ever had soggy

Cheerios stuck between your toes? It's disgusting."

"Ah. I see."

"But the babies don't spit up much anymore. And about the diapers . . . well, I just told Mom and Dad right from the first, 'Hey, don't count on me changing any. You're on your own.' "

She smiled. "So these are the only bad parts about having the twins around? You don't ever feel . . . a little jealous?"

Amber was right. This was getting awfully personal. Besides, Mrs. Van Gent had it all wrong. Lucy and Freddie made me feel special. Nobody else at Nekomah Creek had baby twins. I'd felt almost famous for a while, passing out chocolate cigars to my whole class.

"They must take up a lot of your parents' time."

"Yeah . . . but mostly we all have fun together. I like it."

"Well, good." She took off her glasses and rubbed the bridge of her nose. Without her glasses she looked a lot younger. "And how is it now that your mother's gone back to work?"

Good grief. How did she know all this stuff? Was she some kind of detective on the side?

"Things are okay," I said, wishing I could figure out where she was heading with this. She had her glasses back on and was looking official again. "Maybe a little wilder than before."

"Oh?" She leaned forward. I'll bet she thought it

was like this movie I saw where the mom goes back to work and the dad doesn't know how to do anything so the house falls apart.

But my dad knows how to use a vacuum cleaner. He even showed us how to ride ours like an indoor scooter. And so what if I have to wear dirty socks once in a while? I sneaked a corner-of-the-eye peek at the ones I had on now. Oops—one with red stripes and one with blue. I inched my jean legs down, pretending to be very interested in the Appaloosas in the pasture beyond the office window.

"Can you tell me what you mean by wilder?"

I was trying to concentrate on the horses, thinking how maybe I'd draw them sometime.

"Robby? About it being wilder?"

"Hmm?" I turned back to her. "Oh. Well, ever since the twins it's been wild even *with* Mom. They get into everything, throw the laundry around, stuff like that. I never know what I'll find when I get home."

"I see."

"It's *funny*, though." I was telling the truth and she wouldn't believe me. "I *like* it."

"Please understand, Robby. We're just . . . *exploring* here, trying to find out what's bothering you."

You're bothering me, I wanted to say. I could have been through three more Encyclopedia Brown cases if I wasn't stuck in here.

She made her voice sympathetic again. "Let's try this, Robby. If you could have one wish, what would it be?"

Okay . . .

I took a deep breath. "I wish my mother would get pregnant again"—I stared Mrs. Van Gent straight in her pretty blue eyes—"and this time I wish she'd have triplets!"

□ 2 □

My Dad, the Cook

Thunk.

"Not nice!" Freddie hollered. "Not nice!"

"Oh, no!" I said. "Dad! Look what Lucy's doing!"

From the porch, my sister shot me this wicked, can't-catch-me grin. She'd pushed a jack-o'-lantern off the rail and I could tell by the glint in her eye she planned to go straight down the line, shoving off every last one of the pumpkins we'd just finished carving.

Dad glanced up from the pumpkin he was working on. "Well, don't just stand there, Robby. Stop her."

I made for the porch. Thrilled, Lucy shrieked and danced in her pink boots. I bounded up the steps past Freddie, chased her down the porch, and flung my arms around her middle just as another of our works of art was about to bite the dust. Or maybe I should say bite the mud. Anyway, I hauled her back, getting a face full of her wispy, peanut butter–smelling hair.

"No!" I scolded her. "Bad girl!"

She yelled and kicked her heels against my shins.

"For cryin' out loud, don't hurt her," Dad said.

She wriggled down free. I sighed and rubbed my legs. I can't win. If I let the twins act naughty I'm in trouble. If I stop them, I'm in trouble too.

I zipped up my jacket. The fog had finally burned off, but the big fir trees up behind the house kept all but a few sun rays from reaching our yard this time of year. Besides, dusk was coming on fast. I'd have to hurry to finish my worried-face pumpkin.

"No, Freddie," I said. *"Sharp!* Don't grab my knife . . . Yeah, that's it. You guys play over there." I watched as he and Lucy squatted over a pile of seedy pumpkin goo and started squishing it through their fingers.

Then I went back to my carving, thinking about the counselor today. Amber was absolutely right. Mrs. Van Gent was a snoop. It bugged me the way she talked, hinting there was something wrong with me, something wrong with my family.

No way was I going to tell Mom and Dad about all that, though. Those concerned looks of theirs can turn a little worry into a giant one faster than you can say, "Hey, it's no big deal."

"Oh, look, kids," Dad said to the babies, his voice changing the way it does when he talks to them. He pointed to the old blue pickup crossing the plank bridge down at the creek. "Here comes Mommy."

They stood, faces lighting up.

Then Dad added a joke for me. "Yup, good old Mommy, home from a hard day's work in the salt mines." Actually Mom worked at a print shop in Douglas Bay, drawing designs for stores and companies.

The truck rumbled up the winding gravel drive. Mom slid down from the driver's seat, but before she could even slam the door, Freddie and Lucy were wrapped around her legs, all tangled up and giggling in her long skirt.

"Mom," I said, "you should see what Lucy just did. Dad and I worked hard on these pumpkins and she was just shoving them off the railing."

Mom laser-eyed me. *"Hi, Robby."* It bugs her no end when I launch into a bunch of gripes without at least saying hello first.

"Uh, yeah, hi. But Mom, look what she—"

"Don't worry about it, Robby," Dad said. "We'll just make more."

Mom checked out all the jack-o'-lanterns on the porch and lining the drive. Each one had a differ-

ent face . . . Fierce, happy, scared, surprised . . .

"Just how many more do you think we need?"
she said.

"Come on, we're just getting started." Dad
grinned at her. "A man's gotta do what a man's
gotta do."

She rolled her eyes.

"There's still a lot more pumpkins in the gar-
den," I pointed out.

"That's good to know," she said. "I was worried." She looked past Dad. "I gather you didn't
get to cleaning out the shed."

"Beth!" He pretended to be shocked and a little
offended that she'd even mention this. "Where's
your sense of priorities?"

He uses this word a lot. He says it means knowing which things are most important. On his list,
fun is usually right at the top.

Now I'm sorry to have to say this about my
mother, but she's not like that. Lots of times when
Dad thinks up something neat to do, she just acts
tired and says, "Oh, but it'll be such a mess to
clean up."

At the moment, she was trying to brush the
pumpkin seeds from her skirt. "You haven't forgotten about the potluck, have you?"

"Nope," Dad said. "Cake's on the counter."

"Well, we'd better change diapers and wash
faces here."

Dad wiped his knife on his jeans. "Why don't you find the candles, Robby? We'll get these pumpkins all ready to light and give the little guys a thrill when we come home after dark."

Every year Nekomah Creek School has a potluck and an auction to raise money for special activities. People donate things they've made or don't want, or they promise to chop a cord of firewood or take somebody fishing in their boat. Some things are always the same. My friend Jason Corwin's parents always auction off a weekend at an ocean-front rental condo their realty firm manages, Mrs. Downard offers to sew a dress, and my mom donates one of her miniature ink-and-watercolor paintings.

The auction is a big deal, because Nekomah Creek is kind of famous for having so many people who do really good arts and crafts. So lots of people come up from Douglas Bay on the other side of Tillicum Head. That's the closest real town.

I thought Dad would donate storm windows like he usually does—he makes those out in his shop and sells them to people. So I was really surprised when Mr. DeWeese, the principal, said that the next item for auction was a romantic gourmet dinner for two, prepared by Bill Hummer.

"All *right,* Dad!" I turned to him.

Freddie was standing on Dad's legs, pushing his nose to make it beep.

"Beep!" Dad whispered. I think beeping helped him pretend Mr. DeWeese wasn't talking about him. When he feels shy he does that sometimes—gets real busy with the babies.

"The dinner," Mr. DeWeese was saying, "will feature the finest Northwest cuisine and will be served in the rustic elegance of the Hummers' home, on the banks of Nekomah Creek."

"I didn't write that," Dad whispered to me out the corner of his mouth.

It sounded nice, though, especially if you didn't know that around here, being on the creekbank was no big deal. I mean, so are at least half the houses on Nekomah Creek Road.

Mom and Dad first discovered this place when they were camping through Oregon one summer, back when Dad was a teacher and had summers off. They say their whole future changed the day they pulled their VW van into the gas station down on Highway 101. The ocean looked pretty there, the way the creek spilled into it by Promise Rock, and they decided to stop and grab a bite at the café. A guy there told them about a good campground up Nekomah Creek Road. On the way to it, they drove past the houses and small livestock farms strung up along the creek valley. Dad still likes to tell how he slammed on the brakes when they spotted this old dairy barn with five acres for sale. And up past the covered bridge, the gray-shingled school with its old-fashioned bell tower. Mom says it was as if a vision hit them. They sat by their campfire late into the night, talking about how the barn could be turned into a terrific house, how the kids they'd have could ride their bikes through that bridge to the school . . .

Mom always says this shows that dreams *can* come true because here I was, their kid, going to school at Nekomah Creek just like they imagined.

Dad looked pleased as the bidding for his dinner took off. He's a great cook but Mom's always trying to diet, I'm sort of picky, and the little kids throw more food than they eat. Dad would love a chance to show off his fancy recipes.

So many people were waving their arms, I couldn't even tell who finally gave the high bid. Sixty dollars!

Everyone applauded, including Freddie and Lucy. Lucy looked around to make sure everyone was joining in. She loves any excuse to clap.

After the auction, Mom and Dad started talking to their friends, Berk and Inge Feikart, but their son West and I just nodded at each other and turned away. West and I used to play together a lot. We even have a picture taken down on the beach, each of us nothing but a little round head poking out of our mother's backpack. At their house, we used to have fun chasing under his mother's weaving looms, in and out of his father's pottery studio. But now West always wears camouflage clothes, and he never wants to play anything except G.I. Joe.

So I was looking for some of my other friends when I saw Orin Downard heading my way. I tensed up. Orin's the kind of kid who makes you flinch just walking past. He might poke you or he might not. Either way, you can't relax until he's gone. My mother says he's built like a little brick outhouse. I've never seen such a thing, but I can picture it. No sign saying "Men" or "Women" on it. Just "Orin Downard."

He planted himself square in front of me. "Your father cooks?" The way he said it sounded more like, "Your father eats worms?"

"Yeah," I said cautiously. "He cooks."

He studied me, chewing his gum. "Women cook. Not men."

"That's not true. Lots of chefs are men." I glanced over at my dad. He was wearing his blue baseball cap, the one with the Masterpiece Theatre patch on it. Suddenly I wished he'd gone with his usual stocking hat.

Orin let out this big disgusted sigh. "I'm not talking about restaurants, dummy. I'm talking about people's houses. Cripes, I'll bet my dad could pound your dad."

I squinted, trying to look fierce. "Could not." But it came out sounding puny. And why wouldn't it? It was a lie.

I knew Orin's dad. Everybody did. Elvis Downard. Orin's Grandma had been crazy for Elvis Presley, see, or so people said. Orin's dad was a logger now, but everybody still talked about what a big football star he'd been at Douglas Bay High. Now he drove a pickup with gun racks and a bumper sticker that said, "Sierra Club—kiss my ax."

Orin sneered. "Your dad's a wimp."

I swallowed. I knew I'd never hear the end of this. My dad, the cook.

"Dad?" I said on the way home, raising my voice over the Raffi song that was playing on the tape deck. "Do you think it's weird that you cook?"

"It's *wonderful* that he cooks," Mom said firmly. Then she whispered, "Let's not blow a good thing, Robby."

"If it wasn't for my cooking," Dad said, "you'd all be eating Rice-A-Roni for dinner every night."

Mom and I traded a secret look. We both loved Rice-A-Roni. Also blueberry muffins made from a mix and canned Chinese food. Dad wouldn't touch this stuff though, so we only had it when he wasn't around, like when he went to visit Grandma after her operation.

"But Dad? Is it usually always the mom who cooks?" I know this sounds dumb, but up until now, I'd never thought about it. "Are we the only family where the dad cooks?"

"No," Mom said. "Lots of dads cook."

"Dads around Nekomah Creek?"

Nobody answered.

"Who?" I persisted.

"Sam Logan cooks," Dad said.

"Yeah, but that's because he's divorced now. He has to. I mean dads who cook even though the mom is still there."

Lucy and Freddie were helping Raffi belt out "Ducks Like Rain."

"Quaaaa . . . qua qua qua quack! Quaaa . . . qua qua qua quack!"

Finally Mom mumbled something.

"What?" Quacking ducks can sure make it tough to hear.

Mom raised her voice. "I said, there must be a few men who cook."

Dad laughed. "Look, Robby. In our family, I'm the cook. If it works for us, that's all that matters."

"Quaaa qua qua qua quack! Quaa qua qua qua quack . . ."

Well, if it was okay with him, I guess it should have been okay with me.

But was it?

□ 3 □

Alarming News

Dad stopped the van at the two big fir trees that stood like gateposts at our driveway. He made the rest of us wait while he disappeared into the dark dip where our little bridge crossed the creek. One by one, starting from the house, he lit the jack-o'-lanterns.

"Okay," he said, finally climbing back in. "Are we all ready for a spooky ride?" He cut the headlights.

"Bill!" Mom said.

"Don't worry, I can see."

In the dimness I watched Freddie's eyes get big.

Dad inched the van up the driveway through the drifting ground fog, past the glowing faces. He took it as slowly as he could, but still, it was over too soon.

"Wa mo tine!" Lucy said. That's Lucy-talk for "One more time!"

"Hey, why not?" Dad said. He cranked the car around, drove out over the bridge, and headed back in.

We repeated the little parade, everybody oohing and ahhing. I got in on it too, and at the top of the drive I said, "One more time!"

"No, that's enough," Dad said, unbuckling his seat belt.

Huh. Somehow the babies' magic words never worked for me.

Mom opened the front door and groaned. "I always forget when we've left it like this."

Toys covered the floor of our big main room. The babies had done a shredding job on the day's newspapers and mail. Sofa cushions and extra blankets were strewn around—their morning fort. Over all this the ceiling fan turned slowly, trailing crepe paper and a glob of limp balloons from Freddie and Lucy's birthday party last month.

"Yup." Mom picked up a sprouted potato somebody'd been playing with and tossed it toward the kitchen end of the house. "Looks like rustic elegance to me."

Dad laughed. "Like I said, I didn't write that. Blame it on the auction committee."

"Hey Dad? Are you really going to serve this fancy romancey dinner *here*?"

"Robby, under all this stuff is a perfectly charming house."

"Are you sure?" Mom shrugged out of her jacket. "When was the last time we looked?"

"It's not that I don't like our house . . ." I said. It was pretty nice, really, especially when you thought about it starting out as a barn. Now it looked like most of the other houses along here—weathered shingles blending into the woods. The inside was fixed up with all sorts of recycled stuff —leaded windows from a church in Astoria, maple floors from the old Coos Bay High School gym, and antique brass light fixtures from every place in between.

I picked up a stray rubber band and shot it toward the second-floor balcony. "It *is* kind of messy, though."

"Just looks like we live here," Dad said.

Mom made a face. "*Wallow* here's more like it."

"Relax, Beth," Dad said. "We'll clean it all up and light some kerosene lamps. It'll be fine, you'll see."

"It better be," she said. "For sixty dollars."

Dad and I looked at each other. Maybe Mom was sore because her painting only went for fifty.

Mom pulled Lucy away from her studio door. "Don't even think about it, kiddo."

Lucy flashed her wicked grin. She was coming dangerously close to mastering doorknobs, and you could tell she was dying to get busy on the only tidy room in the entire house.

Mom's studio had to be neat. Her pictures were small and delicate. One fingerprint could ruin an original worth a hundred dollars or more. So it wasn't like an artist's studio you might imagine, with messy oil paints and my mom in a splattered smock. More like a nice, organized office. Sometimes when she got sick of trying to keep up with the mess in the rest of the house, Mom would yell, "I can't take any more of this!" Then she'd go in there and shut the door.

I watched Lucy climb up to join Freddie in leaping from the sofa arms into the remains of their fort.

"When you have this dinner," I said, "what are you going to do with these guys?"

Dad dragged Freddie from the pillow pile and unzipped his jacket. "They'll be the waiters, of course."

"Da-ad."

"Don't you think Lucy would look cute in a little white apron?"

"Mom, he's kidding, isn't he?" With Dad, you never knew.

"Freddie could wear a bow tie . . ."

"You can all go over to Mrs. Lukes's," Mom said. "Why do you think I bid so high on those baby-sitting coupons?"

"Oh." They'd have to clear me out, too. Sometimes I forgot that I was one of the kids instead of a grown-up.

I guess that comes from having been an only child for so long. I mean, I'd been here for *seven years* before these little guys showed up.

And believe me, I'd been wanting a brother or a sister. My mom says being an only child was okay for her, but Dad had four brothers and that sounded a lot better to me. Their house was wild. Dad used to fake nightmares where he'd fall off the upper bunk onto Uncle Fred and pound him, going "Oh, help! Monsters! I'm fighting monsters!"

I wanted a brother to try that on.

Mom and Dad kept telling me they were doing everything they could to get me one. Mom took special pills. When that didn't work, Dad had to give her shots of some super powerful medicine they got in Portland.

Still no luck.

Then one day when I'd practically given up, I climbed down the ladder from my sleeping loft and found them hugging in the kitchen. I was just heading for the stash of leftover Christmas candy, minding my own business, when they kind of gathered me into the hug with them, their faces all glowy.

"Guess what?" Mom had tears in her eyes. "You're going to have a baby brother or sister."

And then it turned out to be one of each! Boy,

did we ever hit the jackpot! Five in our family. That was more like it.

I climbed into my loft now. I had a picture I'd drawn at school taped to the wall up there—me with the two of them. We were all three different. Freddie had Dad's dark curly hair and brown eyes, Lucy had Mom's green eyes, and so far her hair was nothing but crazy tufts of yellow fuzz. And me . . . well, drawing me was the hardest because I'm just kind of average. Average brown hair, average gray eyes. Average height. A little on the skinny side. In the picture we're playing one of our favorite games—Mountain Climbers—where we crawl up the stairs and go avalanching down in a pile of blankets and pillows. I had our eyes all bugging out and surprised as we tumbled to the bottom. "Forevermore!" Mrs. Perkins had said when she saw my drawing. "Your folks let you do this?"

Now, in the loft, I flopped into the pile of stuff I sleep with—a zipped-open sleeping bag, a wool blanket, my old baby quilt, and a wadded-up sheet that had probably stayed tucked around the mattress for about two hours when Mom first put it on. I pulled a book out from under my pillow.

Down below, I could hear Dad talking to Mom in the bathroom while they wrestled the babies into their jammies. He sounded pretty jazzed up about his gourmet production.

"I thought salmon, for sure. And that sautéed

mushroom recipe? The one that calls for the spendy chanterelles? That'd be impressive. They don't have to know we went out and picked them ourselves! Lucy, stop wriggling! We have plenty of frozen raspberries, right? And we ought to get a local wine . . ."

"How about some fancy dessert cheeses?"

Cheese for dessert. Now there's an idea that should have been squashed the first time some lame-brain put it into words. I don't care if Tillamook cheese is a big deal around here. Dessert ought to be chocolate. Period. Oh well, I wouldn't be eating it . . .

After the kids were dressed, Mom started reading them *Home for a Bunny,* one of my old books. I always thought it was too sad . . . that bunny going down the road and down the road, looking for a home. I never let Mom read long enough to find out he got his home in the end.

But Freddie and Lucy like it. I lay there on my quilt, staring at the ceiling, listening. Funny, I'd heard her read this story to them hundreds of times by now, but I'd never noticed before how much that mean old groundhog sounded like Orin Downard. "No, you can't come in my log!"

After the story, Lucy and Freddie padded over and hollered for me to climb down and give them their good-night hugs.

"Well, Robby," Dad said when we had them all tucked in. "This is kind of exciting, isn't it? A fancy dinner for the new Nekomah Creek counselor."

"What?"

"The new counselor," Mom said. "Didn't you notice she was the one who bought your dad's dinner?"

My eyes bugged out. I felt my jaw working but no words came.

"What's the matter?" Mom said.

Dad was watching me with a puzzled smile. He leaned toward Mom. "Looks like a fish thrown up on a streambank. What's the matter, Robby? Don't you have any confidence in your old dad?"

They laughed and turned away.

"Maybe this is her way of thanking you," Mom said to Dad. "She probably realizes it was *your* impassioned testimony that convinced the school board to hire a counselor in the first place."

"You think so?" Dad said. "No, I'll bet she's just interested in fine dining."

Nobody seemed to notice that the gasping fish on the bank—me—was in total shock.

Because I knew the real reason Mrs. Van Gent wanted to come here.

She wanted to spy on our family!

□ 4 □

Pig Snouts and Other Worries

A shadow fell across my desk. I looked up from the picture I was working on.

"Aw, ain't that cute!" Orin said. "Look at all them little animals."

I went stiff.

He aimed a pretend rifle at my picture. "Blam! Blam!"

I jerked my arms across the paper as if his make-believe bullets could really hurt.

"Run, li'l Bambi! Run!"

Mrs. Perkins was frowning over some papers. She had a way of acting real busy whenever Orin goofed off.

Somebody said she was his mom's second cousin or something. Could be. Lots of people whose families have lived around here a long time

are related to each other. So maybe that's why he got away with stuff. Maybe she liked him.

He cackled all the way back to his seat.

Rose Windom and I traded looks. Rose had only started at Nekomah Creek this year, and already she'd had her fill of Orin Downard. No wonder. On the first day, Orin sized up her clothes and said, "Oh, great, another hippie."

He called a lot of us hippies—anybody whose father wasn't a farmer or a logger or a fisherman. He wasn't nice to kids like Jason, either, the ones who lived in big split-level houses and had parents who worked in Douglas Bay. "City boy!" he called Jason.

Why was he like that? Beats me. Most of the

kids didn't much care whose parents did what. They hung around with certain people because they both liked baseball or Nintendo. But Orin kept wanting to sort people out and divide them up.

"You think you can come here and tell us how to run things," he was always saying. " 'Don't cut down them trees, don't go huntin' no more.' "

I never said any of that to him. Those were things the grown-ups argued about. But one time I got mad and I did say, "Hey, I've been here as long as you have. I've lived here all my life too."

"So? Your Grampa wasn't born right here in Tillamook County, was he?"

He had me there. I had one grampa in Southern California and I used to have one in Yakima, Washington. They weren't born here and they weren't loggers.

"He's just spouting what he hears his father say," my folks told me. "Ignore him."

Parents always say that. Have you ever tried doing it?

Lately, I couldn't ignore him. Because now it wasn't just his usual line—*Nobody's as tough as a logger.* Now it was: *Your dad is a wimp and so are you.*

Ever since the auction, I'd been thinking about dads who cook. About dads in general.

I should have just said "Oh, who gives a rip what Orin Downard thinks?" But it bugged me enough that I made the mistake of bringing it up to my friend Ben one day in the cafeteria after Orin had walked by and shoved me.

"Orin's such a jerk," I said. "Tries to make a federal case out of it just because my dad does all our cooking."

Now this is where Ben was supposed to say, "That's dumb."

Instead he said, "Your dad does all the cooking? That's weird."

"*Ben.*"

"Well, don't you think it is? A little?"

Ben's opinion mattered a lot more than Orin's. So calling us weird kind of hurt. Even if he hadn't meant to be mean.

"Why doesn't your mother cook?" he asked.

My peanut butter sandwich stuck to the roof of my mouth. "She doesn't like to." I swallowed hard. "And she's no good at it, either."

"What *does* she do, then?"

"*Ben.* She's an artist, you know that. You've seen her studio at the house."

"Yeah, but . . ."

"And last month she went back to work at the printing shop."

"Yeah?" He twisted the top off his orange Squeezit. "So who's taking care of the twins?"

"My dad. Mostly."

"Oh." He looked like he wasn't sure about this.

I stuck out my chin. "What's the matter with that?"

"Nothing," he said quickly. "Nothing, I guess."

Were we weird? I watched him bite into one of those yummy cupcakes his mother makes. I guess we were different from his family, anyway. They ran this dairy on the other side of Tillicum Head—green pastures full of black and white cows. His dad drove a big old tractor and wore a baseball hat with a John Deere patch on it.

I liked going to the Hammonds'. It wasn't a wild kind of fun because Ben's dad was usually busy working. But Ben's mom was nice and their house was . . . *organized*. And quiet. You could read there. Staying overnight with them was like visiting another planet.

But just because we weren't like Ben's family didn't automatically make us weird, did it?

Next I tried Jason Corwin. His folks were both realtors. They lived in a huge house perched up where they got a terrific view of the ocean. Their place was quiet too, compared to ours. So many rooms, you could never fill them up with noise or mess. Not that I didn't feel like trying! Every time I walked in the front door, I got this strange urge to start throwing pillows around or something.

As far as food, most of what I saw at Jason's house was take-home stuff brought by one of his parents after work.

This time I didn't beat around the bush. "Jason," I said, "does your dad cook?"

"Sure."

Good. Then my dad wasn't the only one.

"He does all our barbecuing in the summer."

"Oh." I sighed. That wasn't the same at all.

Right then Amber Hixon came by with her empty lunch tray. She stopped.

"Don't worry, Robby." She leaned in close to me. "My dad does all our cooking too."

Shock zapped the roots of my hair. She'd been listening from the next table! Watching her walk away, I wished she'd never seen me at the counselor's, because this new buddy-buddy business gave me the shivers. I mean, was it supposed to perk me up that *her* dad cooked? Well, it didn't. Not if her family was the reason she had to go to counseling sessions in the first place.

Now, finishing up my drawing, I was glad when Mrs. Perkins announced that the art teacher was coming the next day and we'd be starting a special project. We were supposed to bring shoe boxes from home to make these little dioramas. You'd peek through a hole and see the scene inside. I thought it sounded great. I put all my worries right out of my mind and started planning what kind of a scene I'd do.

After school that day Rose was waiting for me by the bike racks. Darn. I was hoping she'd forget I promised to stop by her place on the way home. I'd been up there when it was Aaron Stingley's house, and it gave me the creeps. Pretty sad looking, as I recall, and it smelled funny. I didn't like to think of Rose living there.

But she was all smiles. She opened the big cloth bag she always carried. "I forgot. I brought this for you." It was a paperback of one of those Little House on the Prairie books. Looked like it had been read about a million times.

"Thanks." Our school library was not that huge, so I was always glad for more books.

Rose felt the same way. I guess that's how we got friendly so fast.

Mrs. Perkins thought books were important too, as long as you read them during assigned reading time. We had this bulletin board with a paper triangle ice cream cone for each person. Every time you read a book, you got to pin another scoop on your cone. Rose and I had a lot more scoops than anybody else. One day Mrs. Perkins told the class that at this rate, Rose and I would probably be the only ones to earn the reward of real ice cream. Rose and I had looked at each other and gulped, partly proud, partly embarrassed. Think how everyone would hate us if that happened! Ever since then I've been reading tons of books on the sly, only turning in enough book reports to keep Mrs. Perkins from getting suspicious.

But back to Rose . . . She has this long, dark,

tangly hair. Her eyes are big and . . . well, I don't want to sound mushy—I'm only telling you this so you'll know. Have you ever seen sunlight shining through a 7-Up bottle, so green and pretty? Well, that's the color of Rose's eyes.

She has a whole bunch of sisters. You can recognize them because they all dress the same—long flowered skirts and big bulky hand-knit sweaters. When it's cold they wear hats made out of leftover yarn knitted in fancy patterns—like Indians of the Andes in *National Geographic* magazine.

Now some of the girls in my class seem kind of silly. Like Monica Sturdivant, who has to have these little matching kitties on all her notebooks and pencils and boxes of tissue. Whenever I tell some interesting fact I've read, she screws up her face and goes, "Nyuh uu-uh!"

But Rose isn't like that. Rose even likes Encyclopedia Brown.

Kids were streaming past us now, some lining up for the bus, a few unlocking their bikes. Rose's two older sisters headed down the road, and her younger one—the first grader with the baggy tights —waited to go with us. Her name was Cassie.

When Amber Hixon walked by she gave me that smirk again, the one I was beginning to think of as the I-know-something-about-you look. I wished she'd quit it.

She started to go on. Then, like she'd had a second thought, she stopped and turned back to us.

Her chin did that little sticking out thing. "I have to hurry," she announced, "because my Mom's taking me to buy a pony today."

"Wow," I said.

"I already have the bridle," she went on. "It's purple and covered with jewels."

Rose and I glanced at each other.

"Well, they aren't real diamonds. I never said that. Just rhinestones. But it costed a lot anyways."

What could we say? What could you *ever* say when she blurted out stuff like this?

She pushed back her cowlick and jerked her chin again. Then she headed toward a long, shiny car that was pulling up. She'd barely got in before it peeled out.

"I'm not sure I believe that," Rose said as I twirled the combination lock on my bike. "About the bridle."

"She admitted they weren't diamonds."

"Still . . ."

We started down the road, me pushing my bike, Rose's sister trailing behind, banging a rusty Care-Bears lunchbox on her knee. It was a pretty day, the sun lighting up the orange vine maple at the edge of the forest.

"Look out, *girls!*" Orin swooped by on his bike, making us all jump toward the ditch.

"That jerk," I said. My shin hurt where I'd bashed it against my bike pedal.

We walked through the covered bridge without talking, the *bam bam* of the lunchbox echoing behind us. I'd be glad when we were safely up Rose's driveway and out of sight. I didn't want people noticing me going home with her. Maybe she felt funny too.

"Robby?" she finally said. "Do you think you might have an extra shoe box I could use? For the art project?"

"Probably." I was puzzled. "Why?"

She kicked at a rock with the worn toe of her boot. "We don't get many shoes new. In boxes."

"Oh. Well, sure. I'll find one for you."

"Thanks."

We walked some more, then I decided to try her on my question of the day.

"Rose? Does your dad cook?"

She turned those big green eyes on me. "I don't have a dad."

"Oh."

"I mean, I did, but he's gone. I don't remember him cooking though. Why?"

I looked at her a moment. "I just wondered."

But now I wasn't thinking about having a dad who cooked. I was thinking about having no dad at all. Without my dad, our family would have a big hole in it.

"My dad was okay," Rose said, as if I'd asked her. "Not mean or anything. Mom says he just wouldn't settle down."

"Oh." I had never talked to anyone whose dad had up and run off before. I wasn't sure what a person was supposed to say.

"Do you know where he is now?"

"California, we think. My mom's trying to find him because he's supposed to be sending money for me. I hope she does. If I can't have a dad, I'd at least like to have some new shoes!"

My mouth twitched, trying to smile. Nice she could joke about it, I guess. Maybe he left so long ago she was used to the idea.

"Instead of a dad and mom," Rose said, "I sort of have two moms right now. When my mom's friend Shelley got divorced, she and my mom decided to go together and rent a house up here to save money."

"Wow." I pictured my mother double, telling me to pull up my socks, put my stuff away . . . "Two moms. Don't they drive you crazy?"

Rose thought. "No, not really. It's okay. I'd rather have a father . . . If I could have a good one, but . . . actually, it's okay."

"Wait a minute." I glanced behind us and lowered my voice. "What about all these sisters?"

She smiled. "Haven't you heard of stepsisters?"

"Uh, mostly wicked ones."

"That's fairy tales. In real life, mine have been kind of fun." She turned to check on Cassie. "They're not for-real stepsisters, of course, but it probably feels about the same."

I watched her stoop to tie Cassie's shoe. Funny, when you thought about it, the different ways a family could be.

We turned up her muddy drive now. I felt better when I saw the house. The weathered shingle siding was the same, but they'd given the trim a fresh coat of red. Wood smoke curled from the chimney.

I wiped the mud off my shoes and followed Rose inside. I stared. The place looked so different. They'd hung quilts on the walls and draped afghans over the sofas. This wasn't a house—it was a nest! Little embroidered pictures were everywhere. I swear, anything you could do with a needle and thread, these people did.

Now for best smells in the world, you have to put baking bread right up there at the top, and that's what Rose's house smelled like. Her mother was just taking it out of the oven. She cut a thick, hot slice for each of us kids, and poured glasses of fresh-pressed apple cider.

After that Rose showed me her wooden crate bookshelves where she kept her books, and then we went outside. Now that we were at her house, away from the other kids at school, I didn't feel so shy about talking.

Rose stood in the tire swing and spun, leaning back, staring up through the tree branches. "Are you coming to the Halloween party next week?"

"Sure. You?"

"Mmm hmm." She jumped down. "How about your dad?"

"Yeah, he's coming too." I climbed onto the tire. "He signed up to be in charge of the apple bobbing."

"Oh." Rose seemed pleased. I think she likes my dad. She sat with us on the bus for the field trip up to the cheese factory and Dad had her giggling all the way to Tillamook with these coin tricks he does.

I pumped the swing higher, remembering that. Then I remembered something else—Amber, on the bus with us. "My dad does that same trick," she'd said. "And he stays home and takes care of my baby brother just like you do, Mr. Hummer."

Darn. I stopped swinging. I wished I'd quit hearing everything Amber Hixon ever said coming back to me. And wait a minute—*baby brother*? Now that I thought of it, I was sure Amber had said *her* mom was going to have twins. She'd whispered it to me the day I gave everyone chocolate cigars to celebrate Freddie and Lucy getting born. Well, that was two years ago. I'm no expert, but shouldn't those twins have been born by now? She only mentioned this baby brother, and how was I to know? I couldn't remember seeing her family at any school programs, and I'd never heard anybody talking about going over to her house. Amber only mentioned her family in these little bulletins about what they were going to do or buy.

"Your dad is so nice," Rose said.

"Yeah." I bet he would look good to someone who didn't have a dad at all.

And Amber seemed to like him, although I didn't know what she was comparing him to.

But how would he look to someone like Orin who had a dad? A big strong one?

Suddenly, between the swing and thinking about Amber and remembering how Dad planned to dress up for the Halloween party, my stomach felt funny. Before, I always felt kind of proud when he would come in a costume and make everyone laugh.

But now I had to think: What kind of grief would Orin give me when he saw my dad wearing a rubber pig snout?

And what would Mrs. Van Gent say about a grown man with a curly pig tail attached to the seat of his jeans?

□ 5 □

On the Hot Seat Again

Mrs. Perkins's timing was perfect. I was right in the middle of working on my diorama the next Monday when she motioned me up to her desk.

"It's time for your appointment with Mrs. Van Gent," she said when I got there.

I stared at her. "But I talked to her *last* week."

"Come along," she said, and I had to follow her out into the hall.

"Robert, you have to see the counselor more than once to get anything out of it."

"But I don't have anything to say to her. And anyway, I already got the message about not reading so much."

"I'm not sure it sank in. Mrs. Elliot saw you pulling a paperback out of your pocket on the playground yesterday."

"Oh." For Pete's sake, this school was a spy network.

"Besides, all this reading is just a symptom. We think maybe Mrs. Van Gent can get at your deeper problem."

My deeper problem. That sounded so gloomy.

"Now run along." She glanced at her watch. "She'll be waiting for you."

I trudged down the hall. My feet felt so heavy I almost thought I *was* lugging some big problem. Good grief, how could this be happening to me? *Me,* Robby Hummer, who used to be known (I thought) as a pretty good kid.

The door to the little room was open and Mrs. Van Gent was already sitting in there.

"Come on in, Robby. How's it going?"

I gave her a bleak look. How could things be good if I was here?

But at first it wasn't so bad. She started making chitchat about things. I sort of liked it, her asking my opinion about a new movie and if I could tell her the best bookstore in Douglas Bay. She got me talking about a book I was reading. In fact, she seemed so interested I laid out the whole plot for her. I even got up to act out a couple of scenes. That made her smile, and she really did have a nice smile.

Her laugh was even better. She loved the part where I showed how the hero wrestled the python —I was down on the floor—and how it got him

around the neck and he started to choke . . .
"Argh argh argh!!!"

"Everything okay in here?"

I opened my eyes and saw Mr. DeWeese, the
principal, staring at me. I let go of my neck. I sat
up.

"Yes, fine, fine," Mrs. Van Gent said. She cleared
her throat. "Robby was just . . . ah . . . demon-
strating something for me."

"Oh, I see." I don't think Mr. DeWeese saw at
all. He looked at her. He looked at me. Then he
pulled his head back into his office and closed the
door.

"Well," Mrs. Van Gent said as I crawled back up
into my chair. "Well." Her lips pressed together,
but her eyes were still smiling. "Maybe we'd better get down to business."

Now things started going downhill. First she
went over what we'd talked about the week before—me reading so much, me avoiding sports,
how I had to get used to not being an only child
anymore . . .

Then she brought up something new—Dad being unemployed.

"That's correct, isn't it?" she said. "He doesn't
have a job right now?"

"He has a job. He takes care of the twins."

"Of course, and that's very important. But I
meant a job outside the home."

"If he had a job outside the home," I said, "we'd

have to pay somebody else to take care of the babies. That would be a job for them, right? So how come it isn't a job for my dad?"

"Good point!" She beamed at me, surprised. "I can see not much gets past you."

For a moment I felt pretty good, but then she started talking about the stresses on a family when a father is unemployed and the mother is working, how it can be so hard for everyone . . .

"But Mrs. Van Gent? I think my dad *likes* taking care of the babies."

"Well, of course he does, Robby. I'm sure he loves them very much."

But somehow I had the feeling she didn't understand. Dad didn't just love the babies, he honestly enjoyed being the one who took care of them. That's a different thing.

"I think it's wonderful he's willing to pitch in like this until something comes up for him."

I sighed. I just wasn't getting through to her. She seemed to have this picture in her mind of how our family lived, and nothing I said could change it. Maybe that's why I didn't try to explain about Mom getting the money from Grampa Brooks's house when he died, how we weren't rich but we had enough so Dad could stay home with the babies for a while if he wanted.

"He must really have his hands full," she went on. "Do you ever feel he doesn't have as much time for you anymore?"

I looked at her sitting there, so nice and sympathetic. She was *trying* to understand.

"Yeah," I said. "Sometimes." I thought about how he'd promised to play checkers with me the other night after the babies were down, and then kept falling asleep right in the middle of the game.

So I told her about that, and before I knew it, I was sort of complaining how Dad and I hadn't really been able to hang out together since that first week when Mom and the babies had to stay in the hospital in Salem.

I talked about what a great time we'd had then, sitting by the wood stove at night, eating chocolate cigars and listening to the rain beat on the cedar-shingled roof, how Dad told me again about my being born right in our house and my first bed being a wooden apple box.

"He says I'm lucky. I can leave doors open all my life, and when people say 'What's the matter? Were you born in a barn?' I can say 'Yes!' "

Mrs. Van Gent smiled at that.

Then I told how one of my favorite things used to be riding with Dad in the pickup, coming home with a load of firewood we'd chopped, knowing Mom would fix hot chocolate for us. These days Mom used the pickup to get to work. I hadn't ridden in it in ages.

Before the babies, we used to take trips and visit my cousins, but that was too hard now. Heck, we couldn't even go out to eat.

Well, we did once, but between Lucy spilling ice water in my lap and Freddie unsticking somebody else's old chewing gum from under the table and chewing it, Mom and Dad got kind of crabby.

"Okay, I admit it," I said to Mrs. Van Gent. "I wasn't exactly Mr. Cheerful myself. But I still don't think my mom should have made that crack about wishing they'd asked for a table in the No-Whining section."

Mrs. Van Gent nodded sympathetically.

"I mean, how polite can a guy be expected to act with ice water in his pants?" I shook my head, remembering. "The last straw was when Lucy grabbed the hair of the lady in the next booth. 'I'm sorry, Beth,' my dad says to my mom, and he's saying this loud enough for everybody in the place to hear. 'I'm sorry, but this is absolutely the last time we offer to take Mona's kids anywhere!' " I rubbed my heel against my shin. "We haven't been to a restaurant since."

"Is that something you miss?"

"Not really. That doesn't matter at all compared to our trip to Powell's Books. You know, in Portland?"

Mrs. Van Gent's face lit up. "Oh, it's a wonderful store. Are you going there?"

"Well, I want to. Mom and Dad have been promising me we will. I mean, every time I see the ad on TV after *Reading Rainbow* I practically start drooling. You know, where they call it a City of

Books? A whole block? Wow. I've been saving my allowance for months now." I sighed. "We'll never get there at this rate, though. Every time we plan to go something comes up—Freddie gets another ear infection, Mom has to work, the van breaks down . . ." I glanced at Mrs. Van Gent. "I don't blame any of this on the babies, though."

"Of course not."

"I mean, they didn't ask to be born."

Mrs. Van Gent smiled.

"But sometimes . . ."

"Yes?"

"Well, sometimes it seems like I'm always getting in trouble over them. They do something bad and Dad gets mad at *me* because I didn't stop them. I don't think that's fair!"

"No, I can see why you'd feel that way." She glanced at her watch. "Oh, dear, I wish I could hear more about it now but I'm afraid our time is up. Let's remember to talk about that next week, okay?"

"Uh . . ." Right then that didn't sound so bad. Nobody had listened to me talk this long in ages. "I guess," I finally said.

"Oh, by the way . . ." She handed me a paper. "I forgot last week. I'll need to have your parents sign this."

I took the sheet. "What is it?"

"A permission slip for counseling. Just a formality, in your case. I know how supportive your folks were about the idea of having a counselor at Nekomah Creek."

My smile must have looked a little sick. I was thinking they probably liked the idea a lot better picturing Orin Downard in the hot seat instead of their own kid.

Just outside the door, Amber was waiting her turn. As I passed, she stuck her face up so close I could've counted the freckles.

"You didn't tell anything about your family, did you?"

"What do you mean?"

"I mean I hope you didn't get tricked into saying things you shouldn't have."

"I didn't," I said uneasily. "At least I don't think so."

"You didn't complain about anything? About your parents or anything that happens at your house?"

"No!" Why was I lying? Why was I feeling so guilty?

"That's good, because she can be so sneaky. Take it from me, I *know*. She acts so nice, but it's just so you'll spill your guts. Then they get you."

"Get you?" My legs felt weak.

"Yeah, they use everything you say to prove what's wrong with your family."

"Well, I didn't say anything bad about my family."

But as I headed back down the hall, I was kicking myself. Me and my big mouth, complaining about Dad not having time for me, admitting how mad it made me when the twins got me in trouble. I'd probably just turned my whole family in. I pictured Mom and Dad sitting in those little chairs outside the principal's office, hanging their heads. They'd have to wear those pointy dunce hats like you see in old movies. BAD PARENTS, the hats would announce in big black letters.

And it would be my fault.

Back in the classroom, it was free reading time, usually my favorite. Only now, when I opened my book, the words just buzzed around the page. No way would they line up in sentences and march the story into my brain. Already too crowded in there with all these bad thoughts, I guess.

Now that really made me mad! It wasn't enough that the school people were keeping me from reading as much as I wanted to—now they'd fixed it so I couldn't concentrate on reading at all!

□ 6 □

The Spaghetti Disaster

Riding my bike home after school, I felt weighed down with dread. If I didn't have a big heavy problem before, I sure did now. The school would be wanting this permission slip back. I had to tell Mom and Dad about the counselor.

By the time I coasted down over our own little bridge, I had made up my mind to come clean, tell Dad everything, even admit how I'd ratted on our family by complaining to the counselor. I hated to do it, but he needed to know what we were up against.

I took a deep breath and flung open the front door with a bang. "Dad! I have to talk to—"

"Shh! The babies are still asleep!"

"Oh. Sorry, I forgot. But Dad—"

"Will you keep it *down*?"

I winced.

Dad softened his voice. "I'm sorry, Robby, but the kids have been *extremely* cranky today—"

"I know, I know. And they really need their naps."

"*I* really need their naps."

"Okay, but Dad?"

"Dadddeeeee!" The thin wail came from the babies' room.

"Ding-dong it." Dad threw down his dish towel. "I s'pose I better get her. If I don't, she'll wake up Freddie and I'll have both of them on my hands."

He hurried up the stairs, leaving me standing there with my story still stuck in my mouth.

I climbed up into my loft and threw myself onto my pile of blankets. I lay there, watching the raindrops slide over my half-circle stained-glass window.

Dad *didn't* have any time for me. Maybe I was wrong to complain to the counselor about it, but it was true. Didn't seem fair, getting in so much trouble for telling the truth. But I guess I should have paid more attention to Amber when she tried to warn me last week.

Amber Hixon. Exactly why were they sending her to the counselor, anyway? Couldn't be rowdiness. She was quiet. Sullen, you might say. Even when she read aloud she barely muttered. She was always telling me she had a shelf full of books at home, but I don't think she ever read any.

She didn't have one single scoop on her reading ice cream cone. Were they bugging her for not reading enough just like they bugged me for reading too much?

I sighed and rolled over in my blankets. I wished I thought it was something like that—dumb, but not so scary. But when Amber came out of the counselor's that first day, she said it was about some picture she'd drawn of her family. I looked at my drawing on the wall, the one of us kids tumbling down the stairs. Mrs. Perkins had been so shocked when she saw it. Gee, maybe I should've stuck to animal pictures just like Amber should have stuck to unicorns. This *was* about our families. And now wasn't Mrs. Van Gent asking the exact sort of nosy questions Amber warned me she would?

How did I ever get myself into this? How was I ever going to get out?

I thought of my python wrestling match and my cheeks went flaming hot all over again. Had I really done that? But the thing is, when you're making somebody laugh, and they're enjoying it so much, it seems only polite to keep it up, right?

Downstairs, both kids were awake. I guess Dad had decided if he couldn't keep them quiet he might as well crank them up.

I heard my favorite Zydeco record start. That's Cajun music—lots of fiddles and accordions and singing about the spooky black bayous of Louisiana. We like to scream along with the werewolves and zombies in the background. "Zydeco! Zydeco!" the babies are always yelling. That and a lot of French words none of us understands.

Well, I doubt there's a person alive who could keep from dancing when they hear this music.

I hurried down the ladder and swept Lucy up. Now really, I thought, somebody ought to clue Mrs. Perkins in to Queen Ida and her Goodtime Zydeco Band.

Beats the heck out of the hokey pokey.

Maybe I should have mentioned the counselor at dinner, but by then I didn't feel so determined about it, and I hated to spoil everybody's good mood.

As usual, Dad started the goofiness. We were having spaghetti, so he launched into that mushy Italian song from *Lady and the Tramp.* You know, where the two dogs have a romantic dinner and the waiters come out with violins and accordions?

"Thees ees the night, eetsa beauuuuutiful night . . ."

Freddie crooned along, batting his eyelashes, mugging like Dad. What a ham.

So Lucy decided to compete for attention with noodle tricks. Flipping them, twisting them.

Before long both kids were throwing noodles, their little arms jerking out like spring-action catapults.

I cracked up.

"Robby," Mom said in a warning voice. "Don't encourage them."

"I can't help it," I pleaded, clapping my hands over my mouth. Parents are so weird. One time something makes them mad, another time they'll think it's hilarious. How's a kid supposed to keep it straight whether they're in a funny mood or a mad mood?

Right now Dad looked serious. "We've told you over and over, Robby. Just ignore—"

Whap. A glob of noodles smacked him in the eye.

I sucked in my breath.

Dad reached up, wiped it away.

Freddie, flinger of the noodles, was waiting with a hopeful look.

Dad's eyes narrowed. His black brows went together.

Oh, no, I thought. He really *is* mad.

But Freddie was still smiling.

Slowly, carefully, Dad picked up a noodle from his own plate.

Then he tossed it at Freddie!

Freddie shrieked with delight.

"Oh, Bill." Mom looked at the ceiling.

Lucy stood up and squawked for attention, then she dumped her whole bowl over her head.

We all about fell off our chairs. Even Mom started laughing in a tired, I-give-up sort of way.

Through strands of orange spaghetti, Lucy grinned at each of us in turn.

Mom and Dad were laughing. Hot dog! That meant I could laugh too. I wished the counselor could see this. My nutty family! I wanted to make them laugh too.

I picked up *my* plate of spaghetti and turned it over *my* head.

The laughing stopped.

Mom and Dad jumped up.

"Robby! For cryin' out loud!"

Warm noodles were sliding down my neck. Mom attacked me with a dish towel. I guess there was a lot more spaghetti on my plate than in Lucy's bowl. Mom dragged me toward the bathroom.

"What on earth would make you do such a thing?"

"I don't know," I wailed as she made me kneel down and put my head under the tub faucet. Things had gone from good to bad so fast. "Anyway, Dad started it."

She muttered something about bad examples, then lectured me about me being nine and how I shouldn't act like I'm two, et cetera et cetera . . .

But all I could think of was how much I hated shampoos, especially when the shampooing person is mad. Besides, a faucet full of water blasting over your head is pretty distracting . . .

Dad hauled Lucy in, swung her up on the changing table and started wiping her head.

"Poopy!" she cried.

"Okay," Dad said. "But one end at a time."

Freddie trailed in with his favorite stuffed animal, Buddy Wabbit.

Mom started roughing up my head with a towel.

"Hey, take it easy!"

"Spaghetti all over your head." She stopped toweling and looked at me. "What is the matter with you, anyway?"

"I don't know," I said miserably. "Maybe you ought to ask the school counselor."

Dad dropped Lucy's diaper in the toilet and looked at us. "What's this?"

A little warning sign popped up in my brain. *Danger: Concern Ahead.* "Oh, nothing."

"Robby," Mom said, "what about the school counselor?"

I was already kicking myself. Why didn't I keep my mouth shut? Sure, that was neat for a second there, suddenly getting their attention in a real dramatic way. But now they'd want to follow up on it and this was not the greatest time.

I sighed. "They're making me talk to that new counselor at school. The one *you guys* thought we ought to have. They think I've got problems or something."

Mom and Dad looked at each other. They looked at me. I groaned to myself. When they act worried, I start thinking maybe there's really something to be worried about.

"*Do* you have problems?" Dad said.

"Well, some. Like I hate that new jacket you bought me."

"Come on, get serious."

"I am serious. It's too puffy."

"Well, if that's your worst problem—"

"It's not, though! Um . . . Orin gave me a hard time when I brought a boot box instead of a shoe box for our diorama project. He goes, 'You always have to be better than everybody, don't you?' "

"That's nothing new," Mom said. "Orin teasing you."

Okay, *think*. I didn't want to upset Dad, telling how Orin kept talking about his dad beating him up. And I didn't want to hurt his feelings about his pig costume. I had to come up with something safe.

"I'm dreading fifth grade," I announced. "Because they have this plastic model of the human body in the fifth grade and I can't stand thinking about the insides of bodies. You know those wormy things? Intestines? Yuck!"

Dad frowned. "And that's what the counselor wanted to talk about?"

Lucy had toppled the dirty clothes hamper. She stuck a pair of my underpants on her head and paraded around like a queen with a crown, cracking me up.

"Robby?" Mom said. "How about an answer?"

"Oh, sorry." I was still giggling. "What was the question?"

"Daddy fuss it down!" Freddie yelled.

"All right, all right," Dad said, wringing out the diaper.

The big debate over whether I had problems or not had to wait while Freddie enjoyed his favorite spectator sport—toilet flushing. He held his rabbit up for a better view. Every good thing in life Freddie discovered, he wanted Buddy Wabbit to get in on it, too. Lucy joined them at the toilet bowl.

"Watch go down!" Freddie ordered them.

Dad sighed. "What were we saying?"

Mom shook her head. "Wouldn't it be amazing if just once we could have a decent discussion about something?"

"Hey, Lucy," I said. "What happened to your crown?"

Lucy grinned at me.

"Uh oh. Dad, I think she tried to flush my underpants down the—"

Water. Water and worse. Over the sides of the toilet. All over the floor. The babies screaming and running in circles. Slipping in it. Mom grabbing the plunger from under the sink. Dad lunging for the toilet. Dad saying words he shouldn't say . . .

Thank goodness Mrs. Van Gent couldn't see this!

□ 7 □

Playground Showdown

"Now remember our deal," Dad said at the break-fast table a couple of days later. "What are you going to do today?"

I pushed a chunk of French toast through the syrup and repeated my promise in a tired voice. "When I'm out on the playground I'll play with the other kids."

"Good."

Mom and Dad had dragged it out of me why I'd been sent to the counselor, and the next day Dad put the babies in the wagon and hauled them up for a talk with Mrs. Perkins. He convinced her I shouldn't have to talk to Mrs. Van Gent if I didn't feel like it.

But he also agreed I shouldn't be reading on the playground.

"But why can't I?" I said when he and Mom laid down the law. "I thought you'd be on my side."

"Honey, we are," Mom said.

"And Mrs. Perkins means well," Dad said.

"She's actually kind of a nice lady," Mom said. "Don't you think?"

I scowled. Why were Mom and Dad always so quick to point out the good side of everybody *I* had to get along with? Why couldn't I just spout off at somebody I was mad at, like Mom does when she comes home upset about a crabby customer at the print shop? Do you think she'd appreciate me lecturing her on how the guy was probably just having a bad day and he's really a wonderful person underneath it all? No way!

"Besides," Dad went on, "she's probably right— you shouldn't spend your whole life with your nose in a book. When you were little you loved to kick a ball around the yard."

"Well, I don't now," I said.

"But why not?"

I shrugged. Maybe in a weird way it had something to do with having all those scoops on my reading ice cream cone. If you're the best at one thing, it bugs you to be the absolute worst at something else—like maybe people would just be waiting for a chance to make fun of you.

"I think it's stupid," I said, "school people punishing a kid for reading."

"Going to the counselor isn't a punishment," Mom said.

"Oh yes, it is." Boy, Mom and Dad didn't have a clue about all the personal stuff Mrs. Van Gent wanted to pry into.

"Well," Dad said, "we agreed you don't have to talk to her at this point if you don't want to, okay?"

Okay, so I'd play on the playground. But they couldn't expect me to be cheerful about it. In fact, it was making me feel crabby about all sorts of things.

I frowned at Mom. "Did you fix the zipper on my backpack yet?"

"Oh, Honey, I'm sorry, I forgot. By the time I finished the Halloween costumes I was just so tired . . ."

"Mo-om! I'm sick of having to fasten it with those ducky diaper pins!"

Mom sighed. "I never seem to have enough time . . ."

"Orin *saw* those pins yesterday. You should've heard him. He made fun of me in front of everybody."

"Okay, okay, I'll fix it tonight. Remind me, all right?"

I glowered for a moment. "And I'm not going to wear that jacket, either."

"Yes you are," Mom said. "Oh, Bill, look out, Lucy's—"

"Ding-dong it!" Dad pulled Lucy's bowl away from her. "We don't put French toast in our hair."

"I hate that jacket," I said.

Dad rolled his eyes. "Haven't we been through this enough times already?"

"Da-ad! It's too puffy. I feel dumb in it. People'll make fun of me. I won't wear it at recess. I'd rather freeze."

"Oh, for Pete's sake!" Mom banged down her coffee cup. "I haven't had a new coat in three years."

Somehow I sensed this was not the time to say *so what*? But I felt like it. Did Mom not getting a new coat make mine any less puffy?

"That jacket cost plenty," Dad said, "even on sale. We can't afford to be buying things and then deciding we won't use them. Besides, in the store you said you liked it."

"But I was tricked by all those fancy pockets! I didn't wear it long enough to know how it would feel."

"Too bad."

I drew myself up. "That jacket," I said, "makes me feel like the girl in *Willy Wonka and the Chocolate Factory*. The one who puffs up into a giant blueberry?"

Mom and Dad laughed.

"It's not funny! You guys just don't understand."

"Of course we do," Dad said. "When I was your age it was flubby shoes. That's what I called these horrible shoes my mom made me wear. Thick soles, leather. Hey, I wanted Red Ball Jets like everybody else."

I had to stop a moment to get that picture in focus—Dad at my age. "So what'd you do? Fight her?"

"Of course." He picked up a chunk of French toast from the floor and flung it toward the sink. "And then I wore the flubby shoes."

"Oh."

"And lived to tell about it. And now, as a matter of tradition, it's my job to make you wear things *you* hate!"

"Da-ad!"

"And . . . being the dutiful son you are, you're carrying out *your* part of the tradition by giving me a hard time about it. So, isn't this nice?" He slapped his thighs and stood up. "Now. Get going or you'll be late for school."

It was cold on the playground after lunch with no coat. I stood shivering in the foursquare line, wishing I had a nice, warm, broken-in jacket like Ben. Dad should have understood that. He's the same way himself. He *never* likes new clothes. A new coat just looks so . . . *clean.* It sticks out. And then if it's dumb and puffy . . .

I saw Amber Hixon hunched up by the jungle gym. She looked cold too, even though she had on this fake fur vest.

She saw me watching and stared back.

I turned away, tried to shake off my bad thoughts. I wasn't going to the counselor anymore and that was that.

But a minute later I was watching her again. Kind of sick, I know, giving myself the shivers on purpose, but I couldn't help it. Reminded me of coming across a scary movie ad in the newspaper and not being able to stop myself from turning back to look at it again and again.

It was funny about Amber's clothes. She had fancy things. Her jeans had the same label as Monica Sturdivant's, and I knew Monica wouldn't wear anything but the best. But sometimes Amber's clothes were dirty. Or like today, she'd be wearing slip-on shoes with no socks when it was way too cold for that. This was the exact opposite of Rose, whose clothes never had any labels because they were all homemade. But they did the job. Her mom knit those sweaters with the idea of keeping her warm. I don't know *what* Amber's parents were thinking . . .

I inched forward in line behind Ben and Jason, rubbing one shin with my heel, then switching and rubbing the other. I didn't even watch the game. Mostly I stared at the pavement. Hmm—an interesting little rock. I put it in my pocket to use in my diorama.

My diorama scene was going to be Nekomah Creek, with a tinfoil creek and our house in the background. I was using yellow tissue paper over the cutout windows to make it look like cozy lights were on inside.

I studied the ridges circling us, the way the fog drifted in so that only the jagged line of firs at the top stood out sharp. I wanted to make it look like that in my diorama. I wouldn't show the hacked-out part though, the part where they'd clear-cut the old-growth trees and never replanted. My scene would face west, where the V in the ridge-line showed the way the creek ran down to the ocean. For the foreground I was making little clay animals, peeking out from behind the two big firs that stood beside our driveway.

Dad's birthday was coming up and I thought it would make a great present.

"Well, check it out," Orin Downard said, getting in line behind me. "How come *you're* here?"

I shrugged. "Free country, isn't it?" What a joke. The only freedom *I* had was the freedom to choose which game to get creamed in.

All too soon it was my turn. I stepped in the square and rubbed my hands on my thighs. Jason served it up easy to me. I returned it. Actually I hit it three or four times before I went out. Not great, but not total embarrassment either. I got in back of the line, glad to see it was longer now.

Rose came and got in line, then Jason took his place behind her after Orin put him out by slamming one across his corner.

"So what're you gonna be tonight?" Jason asked me. Everybody was excited about the school Halloween party.

"It's a surprise," I said.

Orin sneered. "The real question is, what's your *daddy* going to be?"

"That's a secret too," I said coldly.

"Geesh. How come he always has to dress up, anyway? None of the other parents do."

"Is he really going to wear a costume?" Rose asked.

I hunched my shoulders. "Yeah."

"But I think that's neat."

"Yeah, Orin, so lay off," Ben said. "What's it to you, anyway?"

But Orin wasn't finished. He could play and talk at the same time. "Remember that stupid Star Wars birthday party they had?" This was back when Orin was invited to my parties because he was a neighbor, back before our parents started arguing with each other at county meetings. "His dad actually dug a hole in their yard for the Rancor pit and hid inside playing Rancor Monster. Geesh, that was dumb."

You weren't too proud to stuff yourself with our cake, I thought, my face blazing hot.

"I liked it," Jason said. "And remember his Olympics party? That was even better."

Good old Jason. Nice of him to remember. My folks went all out for that one—a torch-lighting ceremony, track and field events around the yard, a flag-raising ceremony complete with chocolate medals for everyone. Only one problem—I lost every event. Maybe that was the day I decided I didn't like sports. Still, it was a fun party.

"So, Orin," Jason said, "if you're so cool, what are you going to be?"

Orin put a spin on his serve. "Nothing, probably. Anyway, Halloween's nothing but devil worship."

We all gave each other what's-he-talking-about looks.

Then Rose laughed. "That's funny. My mom says it's nothing but *candy* worship."

"Yeah?" Orin chomped his gum. "Well, that's 'cause you're just a bunch of hippies who don't know any better. You probably do weird, sicko things yourself."

"Oh, shut up, Orin," I said. "She does not."

Orin dropped the ball and bellied up to me. "What'd you say?"

I swallowed, wanting to step back but not wanting to look scared. I was, though. I didn't want to punch it out with Orin. He'd pounded West Feikart down behind the alder trees just last month and West was a lot bigger than me. Still, he shouldn't talk to Rose that way . . .

"Repeat what you said, wimp!"

I glanced around at the others and took a deep breath. "I said, shut up. If you don't want to dress

up, that's your business. But I'm sick of you picking on Rose."

Orin fell back. "Oh . . ." He made his voice all
sweetsy. "Robby's got a girlfriend." Then he
started singing it. "Robby's got a girlfriend! Robby's got a girlfriend!"

My face burned. Rose *is* a girl and she's a friend.
But he made it sound like something to be
ashamed of. But if I went "Do not!" I'd hurt her
feelings.

So what I did was . . . nothing. I just pretended
I was suddenly interested in foursquare after all.
This worked, in a way. At least I wasn't getting
pounded.

Orin kept it up. "Robby's got a girlfriend!" He

looked around, trying to get the others to join him, but nobody did. Finally he gave up and went off after Cody Riddle and Nathan Steckler, these two fifth-grade guys he always tags behind.

"Bunch of babies!" he yelled back over his shoulder.

□ 8 □

Hard Hats and
Ducky Diaper Pins

Two o'clock that afternoon—every pair of eyes rested on Elvis Downard, sitting up there in front of the class for Job Day like a visiting famous person.

"Logging," he said, "is the most dangerous occupation there is. They got fancy studies now that say so. Big surprise. More guys get killed out in the woods than in any other job. 'Course anybody who's worked on a logging show could tell 'em that. They don't call those dangling snags widow-makers for nothing." He turned his hard hat over in his big, scarred-up hands. "Y'see, a hard hat's one thing. A big old Doug fir coming at you's another."

You could have heard a pin drop. No smart remarks to Elvis Downard. No way. Everybody had been completely respectful the whole time he told about his job. He was a faller, the guy with the chain saw, the one standing by the tree when it started to go.

I stole a peek at Orin. He saw me and returned a look of calm satisfaction. *Top this,* his smirk said.

I went back to the tree I was doodling on the back of an old math ditto. It was chopped and falling over. TIMBBBEEERR! I lettered. I glanced at the back of Orin's buzz-shaved head. I'd fix him. I drew him into the picture as a little groundhog, running away from the tree, looking back over his shoulder, eyes bugged out and scared.

"Besides trusting the guy working beside you, the next thing us loggers count on is our equipment." Mr. Downard held up his cork boots with the hob nails for walking in the woods. He explained how his pants were cut off with no hem that could catch in the brush. And of course he showed off his chain saw.

Back when I was little, I heard West's dad, Berk, calling someone a logger like it was a nasty name. For a while, I even thought it was some sort of swear word. But my folks finally set me straight. They said Berk just got carried away sometimes. They worried about too many trees being cut down too, they said, but it wasn't fair to blame the loggers themselves. Dad said loggers were just trying to do their jobs like everyone else.

Now, while Elvis Downard was talking, I tried

drawing him. I'd never seen him up close before. His skin was tanned to leather and crinkly around his eyes—all that squinting up at the treetops. His chest was broad behind his red suspenders, and his arms—well, he looked like he could wrestle an elk to the ground by its antlers.

Of course I'd seen him lots from a distance. I had to pass their place if I rode my bike down into Nekomah Creek. Sometimes on the weekends I'd see him taking a chain saw to a pile of firewood logs in his turnaround.

Now a chain saw gets the job done all right, but it sounds awful. Elvis Downard liked noise, though. He had a riding lawnmower to use on their town-type yard. Also a motorcycle, an all-terrain vehicle, a dune buggy, and a bunch of snarly dogs. Seems like the Downards didn't feel they could work *or* play right unless everybody on the road could hear them.

So there were things I didn't like about Elvis Downard. On the other hand, I had to envy Orin this: If you had a dad like Elvis Downard and somebody said, "My dad can whip your dad," you could say, "No, he can't!" and sure as heck mean it.

I wasn't the only one in awe of him, either. The whole class was. And at least for today, Orin was getting a share of this respect too, just for being the son of such an impressive guy. People had been unusually quiet while Orin read his part of the Job Day report.

"That was wonderful, Elvis," Mrs. Perkins said when he'd wrapped it up. "Any questions, class?"

"Mr. Downard," Ben said, "have you ever had any close calls yourself? I mean with rolling logs and like that?"

Elvis Downard showed his teeth in a slow smile. "Don't know anybody who's been in the woods as many years as I have who hasn't."

Darrel Miskowiec stuck up his arm, fingers spread wide. "My dad's a logger, too," he said. "Name's Ed Miskowiec."

"Sure, son." Elvis Downard winked. "I know your dad. Choker setter, isn't he? Risky business."

Darrel flushed with pride, his eyes making a quick sweep of the room. He wanted it understood that his dad was the same kind of tough guy as Orin's.

But I remembered Darrel's dad as nice more than tough. Last year he took our class on a hike to see where they were planting the new trees. He told how Darrel's mom worked at the tree farm, packing up seedlings that were sent out to start the new forests. That stuck in my mind. Thousands and thousands of baby trees. Now there was a job to make you feel like part of something big!

Amber raised her hand. "My dad drives a log truck."

"Does not," Darrel said.

"Well, he used to," Amber shot back. "I've even ridden in one."

Calmly, quietly, Rose put up her hand. "Are many women becoming loggers these days?"

Some of the boys snickered. Elvis Downard just kind of chuckled and scratched the back of his head.

"Frankly," he said, "I don't think there's too many women could handle it. Not too many men, either, for that matter."

I slumped lower in my seat and started another dreary doodle, picturing *my* dad, standing in front of the class, explaining how to do diapers. I cringed at the thought. And then I felt crummy about being embarrassed. I mean, changing diapers is a pretty important job too, right? Just think what would happen if they *didn't* get changed!

Still, when Mrs. Perkins assigned a report on either a job we'd like to do someday or a job our parents did now, it didn't even occur to me to write about being a dad. And I was the one who'd argued to the counselor that taking care of babies was a real job, right?

My report was about being an artist, both because of my mom and because that's what I wanted to do.

I blinked at my doodling. I'd drawn a ducky diaper pin without even knowing it! I quickly scribbled it out.

Rose made a warning face at me. I was getting too obvious with my drawing. I sneaked a peek at Mrs. Perkins. No problem there. She was devoting her full attention to Elvis Downard as he went on with more stories.

"Why, one time we had a guy up there topping a big old fir and it starts to split . . ."

I'd never seen Mrs. Perkins like this—cheerful. I sighed. She wouldn't be wondering if Orin's family was okay, if his father was the way fathers ought to be. Her husband was probably a logger too.

I was starting to wish I'd lied and said I wanted to be an airplane pilot or something when I grew up.

Before, I'd been looking forward to showing off some of Mom's printed-up greeting cards. It always bothered me that only a few gift shops carried them. I wanted more of the kids to see them. But now, as far as my report went . . . Well, telling about painting pictures for art galleries was going to sound awfully wimpy after this. A nice thing for a mom to do, maybe, but not a goal I felt like bragging about for myself. I mean, it isn't the least bit dangerous.

"Thank you so much for coming in," Mrs. Perkins told Elvis Downard when he'd finished. "Class?"

An enthusiastic chorus of thank-yous followed him out the door.

"Now." Mrs. Perkins turned around, all flushed. "We have time for one more report. Let's see . . . Robert Hummer?"

Oh, no. I knew I couldn't do it. Not right after this.

I mumbled that I wasn't ready.

"What's that, Robert? Speak up."

"I said I'm sorry, but my report isn't finished."

Mrs. Perkins's eyebrows went together. She tapped the eraser end of her pencil on her desk blotter, her glow fading.

Go ahead, I thought. Give me any kind of look you want. It's better than having Orin and everybody laughing at me.

I hung my head.

□ **9** □

Halloween Shivers

I was still feeling kind of bummed out when I walked into the cafeteria that night for the party, but I started to cheer up when I saw my costume was a hit.

"How'd he *do* that?" I heard West Feikart whisper.

I was wearing a robot suit of toy Construx pieces. Dad had helped me rig up the lights on it with batteries so I not only glowed in the dark, I flashed!

For a minute I checked out everybody else's costumes while they checked out mine. All West had done was add greasy green camouflage makeup to the clothes he always wore. Also a helmet with ferns stuck in it. Ben was a mummy. Willow Daley had turned her hair punk-rocker purple. Monica

Sturdivant looked totally silly as a kitty, of course, tiptoeing around, meowing at everybody. She sounded like that puppet on Mr. Rogers. "Meow, like your meow costume meow."

Freddie and Lucy—or maybe I should say Mickey and Minnie Mouse—were bug-eyed at all this. They clung to Mom's legs when somebody in a rubber gorilla mask stuck his face down at them and made scary noises.

"Knock it off, Orin," West said.

So that was Orin. Should have known.

"It's just pretend," Mom said soothingly, glancing at Orin. "Look. See, there's Daddy, over by the cornstalks."

Dad had come early to fill up the washtub for apple bobbing. Spotting us, he gave the little two-fingered oink-oink salute he'd been practicing ever since he put on his rubber pig snout. Then he turned around and wagged his curly pink pipe-cleaner tail.

I rolled my eyes. What a nut.

"Daddee! Daddee!" The twins let go of Mom and headed toward him. Mom followed.

By now I didn't feel so worried about Dad's nuttiness. For one thing, Mrs. Van Gent was nowhere in sight. Also, lots of people had crazy costumes. Even some of the teachers.

But not Mrs. Perkins. She was selling tickets for the game booths. Looked like her idea of getting wild and crazy was to wear pants instead of a dress.

The refreshment table was loaded. I'd start with a pumpkin-shaped sugar cookie and go on from there. Carameled apples, doughnuts, popcorn balls . . .

"Robby, you look terrific!" It was Mrs. Kassel, my teacher from last year. She was ladling punch, wearing a headband with two bobbly eyeballs boinging from wires. She gave me a big silver grin.

I don't know why, but I loved those braces of hers. Or maybe it was just her smile I liked, with or without braces. She had a neat voice, too, a little husky, like she was coming down with laryngitis.

"Say," she said, "did you see 'The Far Side' this morning?"

I grinned. "Yeah, that was a good one."

We both liked that comic strip. She always said I had a weird sense of humor for a kid. Sometimes last year when she didn't get the joke, she'd ask me to explain it.

"How's fourth grade going for you?"

"Oh, pretty good." At the moment that seemed true enough. Nobody made fun of me for not being a champion foursquare player at recess, my diorama project was turning out neat, and everybody liked my costume.

"Is that your little brother and sister out there? What a riot!"

The twins had joined the big kids on the dance floor. It wasn't the polka or Zydeco music but it had a beat—that's all Freddie and Lucy cared about.

Mom had made Lucy a red-and-white polka-dot dress out of some curtains she got at the thrift shop, and Lucy was real excited about twirling her stiff petticoats. Freddie had red shorts with two big buttons. He was more into stomping.

Mrs. Kassel watched them, her ladle poised in mid-air. "How did you do those noses? They look so cute!"

"Stove black. That was my idea."

She shook her head, half ready to run out and scoop them up for hugs. I wasn't jealous, though. I already knew she liked me. Maybe that makes all the difference.

See, sometimes I *do* hate it when people carry on over the twins. When we first started taking them out to the store and stuff, it was shocking, how much attention they got. Ladies we didn't even know would come up and gush on and on . . . "How cute! How darling! And *two* of them!" Then they'd push their grocery carts past without ever once even looking at me. What *was* I all of a sudden, the invisible kid?

If Mom tried to kind of draw me into the picture, point out that actually she had *three* children, the other lady would always say to me, "My, I bet you're a big help to your mother." I got so sick of that! Sometimes I felt like saying, "No, I'm no help at all. Actually I'm a big pain, okay?"

There was only one thing worse—the people who paid no attention to Freddie and Lucy at all . . .

"Hey, Robby." It was Jason, dressed as a football player. "Let's go do the darts and stuff. Ask your dad for some money."

I robot-walked over to the apple-bobbing corner. Dad was oink-oinking all over the place, adding apples to the washtub while the kindergarteners laughed and splashed and held their stomachs like they ached with giggling.

"Dad, I need money for the game booths."

"Oink, oink!"

Another burst of giggling.

"It's for a good cause," I reminded him as he pulled out his wallet. After the party was paid for, the extra money would go to the school's Thanksgiving Basket fund. One of the sawmills in Douglas Bay had closed, and this year we wanted to help the families of the people who'd been laid off.

After Jason and Ben and I had done all the different booths, we decided to get in line for the haunted house. But first I detoured by the refreshment table so I'd have something while I waited. I was snagging a popcorn ball when Rose came up to me.

"Your costume looks great," she said.

"Uh, yours too."

She was Princess Leia, with a sheet gathered into a flowy dress and her hair in coils over her ears.

"Where you going?" she asked as I turned to leave.

"The haunted house."

"I'll go with you." She took a popcorn ball for herself and followed. "Um, Robby? Thanks for . . . you know, what you did on the playground today."

"I didn't do anything."

She smiled. "Yes you did. That's the first time anybody's ever taken my side in front of Orin Downard."

"Oh." Jason and Ben were already farther ahead in line. Rose and I got stuck behind this eighth-grade alien who kept bugging the ballerina in front of him.

"Hey, Rose," I said, hoping to change the subject. "Have you ever heard of this huge bookstore in Portland called Powell's?"

She shook her head no.

"Well, it's supposed to be great. A whole block of books. Anyway, my parents promised to take me up there Saturday and I was wondering if . . . well, do you want to go too?"

"Go with *you*?"

"Well, yeah." For crying out loud, it wasn't supposed to be a date. It's just that Dad said I could bring a friend, and I knew Rose would appreciate it. I mean, it'd be wasted on Jason. All he reads is comic books.

"I'll ask my mom," Rose said. "But I'm sure it'll be okay." She bit into her popcorn ball. I could tell she was excited. But then a shadow went over her face. "I wouldn't be able to buy much, though."

"Well, we'll probably go to the zoo and the science museum, too."

"Really? Wow! And even if I couldn't buy any, just seeing all those books . . ."

As the line inched forward, we watched the eighth graders dancing and finished our popcorn balls. Getting closer, we could hear the spooky sounds coming out of the haunted house.

Just as we reached the entrance, Rose tipped her head toward mine. "Did you hear about Amber Hixon?"

My scalp prickled. "Hear what?"

"They took her away from her parents."

"What?"

"My mom heard these social workers came and got her right after school today. Now she's probably going to a foster home."

She might as well have socked me in the gut. "But how could they just take her away from her family?"

"I don't know. My mom thinks it was the school counselor's idea."

A hand reached out from the cardboard door of the haunted house and pulled me into the darkness. It was hot and stinky and I could hardly breathe.

Somebody stuck my hand into a bowl of what was probably spaghetti. "Heeeeerrrreee . . . feel some nice guts!" Then a werewolf popped up in front of me. "Aarrrggghh!"

I wasn't a very good customer, though. All of a sudden I was too busy being scared about real things to sweat the pretend stuff. I was just stumbling along, thinking of Amber's trying-not-to-cry face, the words she'd muttered to me after she came back from Mrs. Van Gent's office the other day. "I swear, Robby," she'd said, "families don't mean nothing to that woman."

A foster home. I'd read about those. That's where kids go if things aren't right at their house. In one book a boy got taken away because his father accidentally ran over his legs with a car. But Amber didn't have broken legs or anything. Her parents had bought her a pony, for crying out loud.

Ahead of us, the ballerina squealed. *I have to get out of here,* I thought, my Construx suit banging against the cardboard walls. *I have to hear the rest of this.*

"Rose?" I said into the darkness. "Rose, are you there?"

I felt a hand take mine. Spaghetti sauce gooshed between our fingers.

"I'm right here. Isn't this scary?"

"Rose," I whispered, "how could Mrs. Van Gent get Amber taken away?"

"What? Oh, well, I guess they just thought her family was too weird."

"Eeeeekkk!" A vampire with a flash-lit face loomed in front of us.

This was impossible. I concentrated on pulling Rose through the maze as fast as I could. Finally we broke into the cooler air of the gym.

"That was fun!" Rose said, her cheeks pink.

Suddenly I realized we were still holding hands. I dropped hers and wiped spaghetti gunk on my jeans.

"But Rose, who's they?"

"Who's they who?"

"Amber Hixon," I said impatiently. "Who thought her family was weird?"

Rose blinked like she'd already forgotten about it. "Oh. Well, maybe it started with Mrs. Perkins and the counselor. My mom says teachers have to report it if they think a kid's in trouble. It's the law. And then there's something called Children's Services. That's the government."

"The *government*? Can they do that? Just take a kid away from his—" I caught myself. "I mean *her* family?"

Rose peered at me. "Robby? How come you're so upset about this?"

"I'm not upset."

"You act upset." She gave me a Concerned Look. "Was Amber your girlfriend?"

"No!" It came out meaner sounding than I meant it to. "I just—it doesn't seem fair, that's all."

She nodded. "My mom doesn't think it is, either. It's supposed to be for the kid's own good, but sometimes . . . Well, she had a friend whose kids were taken away and my mom said it was just because they didn't like her lifestyle."

"What do you mean, her lifestyle?"

"You know, the way they lived. This social worker was always coming around, criticizing her housekeeping, saying the kids would get sick if she didn't keep things cleaner. Stuff like that."

"Jeepers." The teachers, the counselors, and social workers from the government. I never realized they had so much power.

Too bad I didn't have Mrs. Kassel anymore. She thought my family was okay. But maybe Mrs. Perkins figured we were hippies. Maybe she hated hippies as much as Orin's family did.

Suddenly I had an awful thought. I'll bet she suspected my folks had some terrible secret to hide, Dad marching into the school like that and telling her they didn't want me talking to the counselor . . .

"I didn't mean to spoil the party for you," I heard Rose say. "I'll go find my mom and ask about going to Portland, okay?"

"Yeah, sure." Suddenly I just wanted to be near

my parents. I headed for the apple bobbing as fast as my robot suit would let me.

"Oink, oink," Dad said. "How was the haunted house?"

"Okay."

"Must have been scary. You're shaking."

Lucy and Freddie were hanging over the edge of the washtub, poking the apples down with their fingers, giggling as they bobbed back up.

A second grader pushed her face through the water, trying to corner an apple. Her braids were getting wet.

"Brrr! Looks awfully cold."

I turned around. It was Mrs. Perkins, watching us.

Dad grinned. "Doesn't seem to faze them, does it?"

She shook her head. "At my last school, Beaverdale, we always hung the apples from strings. More sanitary, the principal said."

"Mr. Hummer!" Another kid tugged at Dad's shirt. "Is it my turn yet?"

"Hang on!" Dad gave him the little oink-oink salute and turned back to Mrs. Perkins. "Actually, I never thought of that. Maybe next year we—"

"Dad, look out!"

Splash.

"Lucy!"

In a flash Dad scooped her from the tub. "For

cryin' out loud!" he said, standing her to drip on the wood floor.

Lucy sputtered with surprise, then grinned to find herself the center of attention.

"Lucy, Lucy, Lucy." Dad shook his head like he didn't know whether to laugh or be mad.

Her polka-dot dress hung limp over her stiff petticoats and her stove-black nose was smeared. Wet strings of hair were plastered to her cheeks. Dad fished her Mouseketeer ears from the washtub, shook them out, and set them on her head.

Everybody laughed. Even Mrs. Perkins.

"Forevermore," she said breathlessly. "I'm sure glad you pulled her out so fast."

"My reflexes are getting better all the time," Dad said.

Mom came hurrying up. "Oh, dear. I should have been watching her closer. I got talking to Inge . . ." She sighed. "Well, I'll just have to take her home. I guess with Lucy I should always figure on spare clothes."

Then Mom noticed Mrs. Perkins.

"Lucy gets into trouble like this all the time," she said lightly, wrapping her jacket around her. "Don't you?" She made a pretend fierce face at Lucy and kissed her forehead. Then she smiled at Mrs. Perkins. "I'm just amazed we've never had to go to the emergency room yet."

This was where Mrs. Perkins was supposed to

laugh and say she understood and aren't kids the darnedest and all that.

Instead her eyebrows went up.

Mom and Dad glanced at each other, some little message going between them.

Maybe they were scared too. Maybe they were starting to catch on to how dangerous it could be to get on the bad side of someone like Mrs. Perkins. Someone who had more power over us than I ever realized.

Suddenly I wanted to crawl under the punch table. I had the strangest urge to just sit there and read some Encyclopedia Brown. Why couldn't I be like him? He's smart and all he does is solve crimes. He never wastes time worrying about personal muddles.

No wonder I like books better than real life.

□ 10 □

Tough Times for a Failed Hero

All the next morning I sat there in class, staring at Amber Hixon's empty desk. Funny. Until she came out of Mrs. Van Gent's office all red-faced that first time, I'd never thought much about her at all.

Of course there'd been times over the past couple of years when you couldn't help noticing her, like in first grade when she was the only one who came to school on Halloween without a costume. Our teacher took out some scarves and bracelets and helped her dress up like a Gypsy. But Amber just stood there, not even cracking the teensiest smile, never thanking Mrs. Murphy. "My mother made me a beautiful bride dress," was all she said, "but it turned out too nice to wear to school."

In third grade she sat right in front of me. I spent a lot of time looking at the back of her head, wondering if she knew her hair was all snarled up. Why didn't her mom make her comb it? Don't get me wrong—personally, I hate to be nagged about that kind of stuff. It'd be weird, though, if my parents didn't.

Now Amber was gone, and I was thinking about her a lot more than I ever had before. What was happening at her house that made the counselor think she ought to live somewhere else?

When I got home that afternoon, Dad said the kids'd had a rough day. At first he thought maybe they'd just gotten into too much Halloween candy, but now they had fevers and it looked like the flu. He'd already called Mom and told her she'd better come on home if she could.

So we were all there when Freddie first got that stricken, cross-eyed look. Then he reared back and heaved all over Buddy Wabbit.

Shocked silence.

Mom was the first to spring into action. "Grape juice," she said, picking up the bunny with two fingers. "You gave him grape juice." She yanked a long strip of paper toweling out of the holder and started swabbing at everything, including Dad. "This'll stain like crazy."

Holding Freddie, Dad wiped his dripping hand on a towel. "The clinic said liquids."

I came to Dad's defense. "Freddie wanted it, Mom. Really. That's all he'd take."

Mom looked at Freddie and her face softened. "You poor little guy. Don't you worry. We're going to get you all fixed up."

"Buddy!" Freddie noticed his bunny was splotched purple. He stretched his arms out and screamed. "Buddy Wabbit!"

"Let me get him cleaned off, Honey," Mom said, "and then you can have him back."

"Nooooo! Buddeeeeeee!"

"Oh, let him have it," Dad said. "If it'll stop him crying."

But when Mom tried to hand it to him he got even more upset. "Buddy Wabbit! *No* Buddy Wabbit!" He wanted him but he was grossed out at the same time. Finally Dad carried Freddie off to the bathroom to clean him up.

Lucy toddled in with the end of a roll of toilet paper and started mopping at everything, just like Mom.

"Oh, no!" I said. "Look, Mom. The other end's still attached in the bathroom! She's undoing the whole roll!"

"Fine. Whatever. I don't care right now." Mom was frantically working on Buddy. After a moment, she stopped and gave Lucy a quick smile. "You're a good little helper, aren't you, Honey?"

"Helper," Lucy said. Then *she* threw up.

"Oh, no!" I shrieked, making for the bathroom. "Dad!"

"For Pete's sake, Robby. Yelling loud enough for

the neighbors to hear doesn't help. How about giving us a hand?"

"I'm trying!" I protested. "But how'm I supposed to know what you want me to do?"

Mom came in with Lucy and started peeling off her clothes.

"Buddy!" Freddie screamed. "Buddy Wabbit!"

"Go clean up Buddy Wabbit, why don't you," Dad said.

"Me? But . . . Dad, he's all . . . vomity."

"I *know,* ding-dong it! The whole house is."

"I'm not," I offered, like maybe this fact would excuse me.

"Go!"

"All right, all right!" He didn't have to be so mean about it.

I picked Buddy Wabbit up by his cottontail and carried him to the kitchen, scrunching my nose sideways to keep out the stink. I set him on the counter and studied him.

You'd hardly recognize him as the soft, fluffy fellow I'd picked out in the hospital gift shop the day Freddie and Lucy were born. Amazing, the difference between him and Lucy's bunny, who still sat clean and unloved on the shelf. Mom worried that Lucy wasn't very motherly, but maybe her bunny'd lucked out. Because Freddie being so superfatherly had been pretty rough on old Buddy Wabbit. When a kid never lets go of a bunny, every possible thing gets spilled and smeared on him.

"You're gross," I said. "You know that?"

Now I knew better than to dunk that bunny in the sink. Dad tried that on a bear of mine once and he never did get dry inside. Poor old Bunky Bear. Rot City. No, this was definitely an outside job. I found this can of upholstery cleaner Mom uses, shook it up and let 'er rip. I laid a long blob of foam down his back and then, like the directions said, went at him with a damp rag.

That stuff worked pretty well. When he was clean I took him into the bathroom and got out my mom's blow dryer.

"Good thinking, Honey," Mom said.

"Now we're cooking with gas," Dad said. "Sorry I yelled, Robby."

"It's okay." I understood. When babies yell, it makes everybody want to yell.

Freddie hadn't let up on wanting his Buddy, but now it was more like a steady whimper.

"Buddy . . . Wabbit . . . Buddy . . . Wabbit . . . Buddy . . . Wabbit . . ."

"Hang in there, Freddie," I said as I blasted Buddy with hot air. "He'll be ready in just a minute."

Mom and Dad gave each other this look that means they're feeling pleased with me. All right. The babies were cleaned up and the general hubbub had calmed down quite a bit. With me pitching in, things were under control.

"Now Mom," I said. "We've got to vacuum this

guy. I read the directions. You've got to suck all the dried soap off. It's strong stuff. Makes you cough. We don't want the babies breathing it or eating it or anything."

"Okay. Whatever you say."

We all went out in the main room and she attached the hose to the vacuum.

"Do you want me to do this part?" she said.

"No! No, really." Just look at Freddie there, watching me with those puppy dog eyes, counting on *me,* his big brother, to save the day. Was I going to let my mother have the final glory? No way!

Freddie seemed doubtful when he got the idea something serious was going to happen between his Buddy and the vacuum cleaner. But I guess he had a lot of faith in me because all he did was pull his finger out of his mouth and say, "Buddy?"

"Don't worry," I said in my most reassuring voice. "He's going to be fine."

I sat with Buddy clamped between my knees. Mom pushed the power button.

"Now be careful," she said over the roar. "That has a lot of suction."

"Yeah!" I shouted. "Look what a great job it's doing." The suction was just fluffing that old matted fur out like nobody's business.

"Watch out for the ears," Mom said.

"What?"

"I think one of the ears is loo—"

Shloop.

"Buddy!" Freddie screamed, horrified.

"Oh, great," Dad muttered.

"I couldn't help it!" I cried, staring at the one-eared bunny. "It happened so fast. I was just going along—"

"Take it easy," Dad said.

"I never do anything right!"

Mom shut off the vacuum.

Freddie screamed and screamed. It was the same story all over again. He wanted his Buddy but not if he didn't look right.

I started to cry. I couldn't help it. I'd come so close to being Freddie's hero.

Mom gave me a squeeze. "It's okay, Honey."

"No, it's not! Look at him." Freddie was having an all-out fit.

"He's not feeling good, that's all. We'll fix his bunny somehow. He'll cheer up."

But Freddie didn't feel like cheering up. He felt like *throwing* up.

All over Lucy.

Well, I don't even want to talk about the rest of that night. I just tried to keep out of the way. Long after I was in bed I could hear my parents snapping at each other. You know how it is. The words themselves weren't so mean, but the way they said them was.

"No, I haven't taken his temperature again. Have you?"

"I was just *asking,* okay?"

And once when I looked down out of my loft, I saw them picking through the ripped-open vacuum cleaner bag, hunting for one dirty bunny ear.

In the morning the babies were playing quietly for once, dropping blocks in their shape sorters as if the flu had taken all the spark out of them. Freddie had Buddy in tow, I noticed. Somehow, Mom had found that ear and stayed awake long enough to sew it back on.

"Good job, Mom," I offered as I sat down with her at the breakfast table. Anybody could see she needed some encouragement.

She was still in her flannel nightgown with her elbows propped on the table. Her eyes were red and her hair . . . well, I'll bet she never would have gotten it frizzed in the first place if she'd realized how it was going to look on mornings like this. She smiled at me in a tired way and took another sip of coffee.

I sat there looking at my cold cereal, not really hungry, but grateful for the feeling of peace in the house.

"Hey, you over there," Mom said to Dad. "Father of this brood."

Dad lowered his newspaper. "Who, me?" His eyes were at half mast.

"Yeah, you." She squinted at him. "Guess

what." Her face slid into a slow, crooked smile. "I've been thinking and I've decided something."

Dad cocked his head my way. "Uh oh."

"I've decided I can't think of anyone I'd rather be going through all this with than you."

"Oh, yeah?" Dad winked at me. "Gee, I can think of lots of guys I'd rather you were going through this with than me."

Mom drew back like he'd hit her.

I cringed, too.

"Joke!" Dad said quickly. "Joke!"

They'd come so close. Almost back to talking nice again and Dad had to go blow it.

"Oh, come on," he said. "It was just a joke."

But she was already crying. "I'm too tired for jokes!" And then she staggered up the stairs.

The babies stood up and stared after her. Then *they* burst into tears.

I felt like crying, too.

"Well, gee," Dad said. "Looks like I'm in the doghouse now."

I nodded. This was the most upset Mom had been since Dad gave her a valentine with a big ugly pig on it last year. Dad and I picked it out together. I thought it was pretty funny, but I guess she was hoping for hearts or something.

"I've got to get to school." I stood up.

Only I didn't make it to school. I didn't even make it to the door. But since I'm nine, I did make it to the bathroom.

□ 11 □

Little Purple Fingerprints

Only one thing looks sadder than a molding jack-o'-lantern sitting in the rain—face collapsed, insides black and gunky—and that's twenty-two of them.

I turned away from the window and fell back into a pile of newspapers on the sofa. I could hear Dad on the phone, telling Rose's mother that everyone was sick and we wouldn't be going to Powell's Books after all.

"I'm never going to get to go there," I said when he'd hung up.

"Yes, you will, Robby."

"No, I won't." I scowled so hard my eyebrows hurt from being jammed together.

"Okay, you won't."

I sat up. "I won't?"

"Oh, for crying out loud! Look, Robby, I'm really sorry everybody got sick but that's just the way it goes."

You know those times when it's about five o'clock on a rainy Sunday afternoon? People are cranky because they're hungry but there's no good smell of dinner coming from the oven? The games and toys are in a million pieces all over the floor, nothing seems fun, and the light from every window is a dreary gray? Well, that's how it was all weekend long.

Even Dad got sick. A couple of times he tried to perk people up with a snappy Zydeco record, but it just seemed like a bad joke with everybody lying around like a bunch of rag dolls.

I kept thinking about those television ads for aspirin and cold medicine. They never say, *Hey, kids, being sick is fun,* but they do make it look cozy. Like when the kid comes in out of the rain and the mom tucks him in bed with nice clean sheets, brings food on a tray, and puts her hand on his forehead with this worried, lovey look.

Maybe Mom likes those commercials too, because sometimes she acts that way. When people first get sick, she knocks her lights out being nice, trying to make them feel better. Her voice is as sweet and smooth as cough syrup—almost enough to make you glad you're sick. Trouble is, this only lasts a couple of hours, three at most. Then she gets kind of crabby and starts acting like, *Okay, you can get well now.*

This time, all the niceness got used up on the twins the very first night. What I got was, "Here's a bucket to put by your bed in case you can't make it to the bathroom in time."

Sunday night I was feeling better, sitting on the floor, sketch pad on the coffee table. The little guys were emptying a basket of magazines while Mom cleaned up the kitchen. Dad sprawled on the sofa, feet propped on the other end of the coffee table. He was finishing the Sunday papers, keeping an eye on the TV news at the same time.

On the screen, they were showing a mountainside where all the trees had been chopped down.

"Look at that, Dad."

"Hmm?" He lowered his paper.

"Even if loggers *are* just doing their job, I don't see how we're supposed to feel good about the forests all getting hacked down."

"Yeah, well . . ."

"I mean, look at that! It's ugly!"

"Hey, you don't have to convince me, Robby."

"Then how come you stick up for those guys?"

Dad looked puzzled. "Do I?"

"Yeah, it seems like it."

"Well, I don't really mean to. Maybe it's just that we don't want you to get the idea that everybody in the timber industry's some kind of villain, that's all."

"Okay—name somebody who isn't."

Dad thought. Then he smiled. "Ever hear of Stoney Halliday?"

I cocked my head. "Is he Scotty Halliday's Great Grampa or something?"

"That's right. And you've heard of Halliday Tree Farms? Well, Stoney started his own sawmill years ago. He bought up logged-over timber lands and replanted them. There's thousands of acres right in this county growing strong young trees now thanks to Stoney Halliday."

"Gee."

"Nobody can tell me a man like that doesn't love trees. Or care about people. Takes a lot of looking ahead and thinking about others to plant trees that won't be big enough to cut in your own lifetime. He's even got a scholarship fund set up. Do you realize that any kid in the Douglas Bay School District who gets accepted to Oregon State can get a full scholarship from the Hallidays?"

"Really? Why'd he do that? Just to be nice?"

"That's about the size of it."

"He must be really rich."

"He is, but you'd never know it to see him around Douglas Bay. Drives a pickup older than ours!"

Wow. That was a new one to me. I thought rich

people were all like that guy who buys everything in New York so he can stick his name on it.

I went back to sketching as the news droned on. It was going to rain, the weatherman said.

So tell me something I *don't* know . . .

Then I heard the announcer say something about Children's Services.

My head snapped up.

On the screen were a lot of people at some sort of meeting.

"This has gone too far," one woman was telling the official-looking people up front. "These are our children!"

Another woman was crying, telling how her baby had been taken away and she wanted him back.

My heart started pounding. "Dad, what is this?"

"Hmm?"

"This news story. What are they talking about?"

"Oh. Well . . ." He watched for a moment. "Social workers, I guess. Whether they've been going overboard lately, taking kids away from their parents."

My mouth went dry. "Have they?"

"I don't know. These folks sure think they have."

I couldn't take my eyes off the screen. Little prickles were zipping up and down the back of my neck.

"But why?" I said. "They don't say *why* they took the kids away."

"Yeah, well, that's TV news for you. Sound bites, they call it. A quote here, a quote there. You don't begin to get the whole story. About this, the timber controversy, or whatever it is. Makes it hard to know which side to take. Or if there's something somewhere in the middle."

"Well, do you think that if—"

A horrible shriek. It was Mom, standing in her studio door.

Dad and I jumped up and followed her into the studio. The busy babies had struck again. They'd got into the tubes of watercolor paints. Little purple and blue fingerprints were everywhere.

Mom moaned, holding up her newest original. Ruined.

She whirled on me. "Robby, I've told you a million times to close the door. Just look at this!"

"But Mom, I—"

"You were the last one in here. Wasn't that some of my sketching paper you had out there?"

"But I closed the door."

"Not tight enough, obviously!" She wadded the wrecked drawing, hurled it into a wastebasket, and marched out. "Do you realize how many hours of work I just lost?"

"But why's it always *my* fault?" I yelled after her. "I'm not the one that smeared paint around!" I stomped out of the studio and threw myself on the sofa. I felt like bawling, but now that I'm nine, of course I had to act mad instead.

Freddie and Lucy had stopped their magazine trashing and stood up, scared by the commotion.

Mom glared at me. "The babies are too little to know any better."

"No they're not," I said. "Look at her."

Lucy whipped her stained hands behind her back with a guilty grin.

"Stop arguing," Dad said. "The damage has been done."

"But why's it always MY fault. No matter what happens, it's MY fault. When they're nine and I'm . . ." I paused to count . . . "sixteen, everything'll still be *my* fault. I guess it was just my fault I was born first, huh?"

"Okay," Dad said. "Mom doesn't need this now."

"Hey, I feel bad her picture got wrecked too. But Dad, I'm sure I closed the door."

"Right."

"I did! Why won't anybody believe me?"

"Robby, that's *enough!*"

I went up in my loft and I didn't come back down. I lay there the rest of the evening trying to read, but mostly thinking mean, mad thoughts.

I halfway wished Children's Services *would* take me away. Then Mom and Dad would be sorry. They'd think of all the things they'd been unfair about. I hoped they'd feel real guilty. Maybe they'd even be on TV, pleading to get me back. I pictured their tear-streaked faces. Yeah, I might kind of enjoy that.

If only I knew for sure they'd get me back.

□ 12 □

Great Whopping Lies

I had never understood how Mrs. Van Gent knew so much about our family—the twins, my mother going back to work, my dad staying home.

Now, sitting in class again on Monday morning, looking at Amber's empty desk, I worried. Did Mrs. Van Gent have secret ways of finding out about all the arguing and yelling at our house?

And Mrs. Perkins—I just hated having to give her Dad's note saying I'd been sick. She probably guessed the twins were sick too. Probably figured it was because of the apple bobbing.

Well, I'm no dummy. I could see where all this was heading. I had to do something about this, and quick.

I went up to Mrs. Perkins's desk. I watched her

frown as she stamped each math paper with a smile face.

"Mrs. Perkins? Today's the day Mrs. Van Gent comes, isn't it?"

Stamp. Flip. Stamp. Flip. "That's right. Why?"

I lowered my voice to a whisper. "I was wondering if I could talk to her."

She stopped stamping and slowly raised her eyes to mine. "You *want* to talk to her?"

I nodded.

"But your father made such a point of saying you didn't have to."

Hoo-boy. I looked away from her, then back. "Well, I changed my mind about it. And my parents don't *mind* if I see the counselor if I want to." I added this part in case she was still thinking they were trying to hide something.

She sighed and shook her head. "I sure do have a hard time keeping up with you, Mr. Hummer."

"Well, Robby, this is so nice to see you again." Mrs. Van Gent gave me her most encouraging smile. "Your teacher says you wanted to talk."

"Uh, right."

"Did you think about the things we talked over last time?"

"Yes, I did," I said, trying to sound confident. "I know you were worried about me, so I just wanted to let you know that everything's going better for me. I've been playing outside at recess. Games. Regular sports."

"And how is it?"

"Not so bad." This was the truth, anyway. "I thought people would make fun of me, but they didn't."

"I'm so glad to hear that."

I nodded, rubbing my shin with my heel, trying to think how to plunge into the not-so-true stuff.

"Um, you might have heard about a picture I drew. Just a silly thing where I'm falling down the stairs with the babies. I didn't want you to worry about that because it's not true. We don't really do that. My folks would never let us. It's just sort of a fantasy—you know, like unicorns."

"Oh. Well, actually, no, I hadn't heard about that."

"Oh." A lie for nothing. "Uh, things are going great at our place. My dad's spending lots of time with me. And he's really cleaned up his act. The house is . . . just perfect now. Clean. Everything where it's supposed to be. One day last week when I got home he had fresh chocolate chip cookies right out of the oven for me."

"Mmmm. That sounds nice."

"Uh huh. And uh . . ." I cast around for more good stuff to say. "Oh. My parents are never fighting. No yelling, ever. And the babies, they've been great. The other day, right out of the blue"—I

snapped my fingers—"they potty trained themselves!"

"Really."

Mrs. Van Gent was starting to look skeptical.
Maybe the potty lie was too much. Well, great. She
didn't believe me when I told the truth and she
wouldn't believe me when I lied either.

But I was in too deep to back out now.

"The other good thing," I said, "is that my dad
has a new job."

"That *is* good news. What kind of a job?"

"Uhhh . . . a carpenter's job. Yeah . . . he's
going to build houses."

She was smiling now. Maybe she did believe
me.

"You know, you're a very special boy, Robby. I
hear all the kids' problems, but not many would
take the trouble to let me know when things start
going better. I appreciate that."

Now it's rotten when somebody says you're bad
when you're trying to be good—like my mom yelling at me about leaving her studio door open when
I *know* I closed it—but it feels even worse when
somebody heaps praise on you for being good
when you don't deserve it.

I guess that's why my stomach was doing funny
things right then. Mrs. Van Gent just sitting there,
looking so pretty, smiling at me so nice.

"By the way," she said, "my husband and I are
really looking forward to the gourmet dinner your

dad's doing for us. It'll be a great chance to meet your parents."

My stomach knotted. *Check on your parents,* that's what she meant. I swallowed hard and nodded.

"My dad's really a good cook," I said. Then I added the biggest whopper of all. "Of course my mom'll have to help him."

□ 13 □

A Heck of an Honor

On Wednesday, just after recess, Mrs. Perkins called me up to her desk.

"I've got some exciting news for you, Robert. All the teachers have looked over the dioramas. They've looked over the art projects from the other grades too. Everyone thinks yours is the best."

"Gee." Some kids coming in were overhearing this, so I felt pleased and embarrassed at the same time.

"We all agree you've completely captured the feeling of Nekomah Creek."

"Really? Oh, I don't think so at all. I wanted to, but how can you without sounds? I mean like the wind in the trees, and the way the little creeks sound rushing down the—"

"Of course, of course," she said, "but we all think it's so cute, the way you even used those bitty electrical bulbs for lighting. Now, you know Mrs. Appleman?"

I nodded. She was the sixth-grade teacher and pretty old.

"Well, she's retiring and we thought it would be so special to give her something to remember Nekomah Creek by."

"Yeah . . . ?"

"So your project is the one we've chosen!"

I stared at her. "You want to give my diorama to Mrs. Appleman?"

"That's right. Aren't you proud?"

"Uh, I guess so, but . . ." I looked around. I wished Orin's desk wasn't so close. I lowered my voice. "I was planning to give it to my dad."

"Oh, you can always make another one for him. And just think, this is quite an honor. We'll give it to her at an all-school assembly."

Mrs. Perkins was smiling at me like she never had before. Somehow I couldn't look at her. I rubbed my shin with the heel of my other shoe.

"I have to admit," she said, "I'm really proud it's one of my students whose project was picked."

I nodded, not knowing what else to do. Then I went back and dropped into my seat.

Maybe all this should have made me feel good, but it didn't. Nice that the teachers liked my diorama, but taking it away from me didn't seem like much of a reward.

And what would I do about a birthday present for Dad? I didn't have time to make another diorama. Besides, anyone knows you can never do something like that the same way twice. Even if I could, I didn't have any more of the lights from my robot costume to put in a new one.

I buried my face in my hands. If I had any guts I'd have told her to forget it. But I couldn't do that, not the way things were. I had to stay on her good side.

"Oh, too bad," Orin said to Darrel Miskowiec. "It was for his daddy."

His voice was right at my ear now, close enough I could feel his breath. "If it's for your dad," he said, "how come you didn't put him in it? You coulda stuck him out front of the house there in his apron, hanging up the laundry."

"Shut up," I muttered.

"Boo hoo," Orin said. "Boo hoo."

I felt something poking my arm. I moved my hand away from one eye.

"Here's a little horsey to cheer you up," Orin said. "Since you like girlie things so much."

I stared. He was nudging me with a little lavender pony. It had a flowing mane and tail.

It wore a purple bridle studded with rhinestones.

"Orin Downard." It was Mrs. Perkins. "Please

get back in your seat and keep your hands to yourself." Then she came around from behind her
desk. "What's that you've got there?"

Orin hid the horse behind his back. "Nothing."

Wordlessly, she held out her hand.

"Just somebody's stupid 'My Little Pony,' " Orin
said, giving it to her.

"Where'd you get this?"

Orin kept his eyes on the floor. "Amber Hixon's
desk."

"You took it from her desk?"

"Well, she's gone, ain't she? Don't look like she
wants it."

Mrs. Perkins held the little horse in her hands.
She looked sad as she gave the flowing mane one
long, thoughtful stroke. Then she turned on her
heel.

"We'll see Amber gets this," she said, and put
the pony in her desk drawer. "And you," she said
to Orin, "had best keep your hands off of other
people's things."

Orin slid back into his desk, surprised that Mrs.
Perkins seemed so upset about the toy horse.

Well, it upset me too, somehow. I kept thinking
about that purple bridle, about those rhinestones . . .

□ **14** □

Please Pass the Kazoos

"Great news!" Mom said when she burst in after work Friday night. She picked me up and swung me around. She hugged the babies. Then she threw herself at Dad.

"Galaxy Greetings accepted the card ideas I sent them!"

"They did? Beth, that's terrific! That's the big company in Ohio, right?"

"Uh huh, and listen to this." She tossed her jacket on the sofa. "They want me to develop an entire line for them!"

"Well, hey!" Dad said. "This calls for a celebration."

"You better believe it. We might be talking about a lot of money."

"Sorry I don't have any champagne on hand.

Will this do?" He started pouring apple juice into wineglasses for everybody. We clinked them, even the babies, and Dad said, "To Mommy!"

"To Mommy!" I said.

"To Mommy, to Mommy," Freddie and Lucy echoed.

Then Dad served up the pot roast.

"Do you all realize what this means?" Mom said. "I can stay home more, work in my studio. I've talked it over with Lynn. It's okay with her if I only come into the shop two or three days a week."

"I thought you wanted to work full time," Dad said.

"So did I, but it's been driving me crazy. I'm tired and I'm cranky and besides, I miss you guys." She looked at Dad. "I didn't go to all that trouble to have these kids just to miss out on all the fun stuff."

Now everybody was in a good mood.

When Mom was all talked out about the greeting card business, Dad started telling about the stuff he'd bought for his gourmet dinner next week. His plan was to get everything ahead except for the things he had to buy fresh.

"I'm not worried about the food," Mom said. "But what about the house? I think we need a week just to clean it up."

I glanced around. Disaster City. Even by our standards, this was a real low. Toys, food crumbs, you name it—it was all over the floor. A lot of the stuff looked like it'd been in the garbage at least once already before somebody—two little somebodies, I should say—flung it out. One of my socks trailed down in front of the TV screen.

"It's on my list." Dad headed for the sink with his plate. "Tomorrow morning, major shovel-out."

"Whatever you say," Mom said, like she'd believe it when she saw it and not before. Then she went over and started cleaning up the kitchen.

Dad blew the animal crackers off the record player and put on Raffi. Then he kicked back the braided rug and some of the toys, passed out the kazoos and we started dancing around. Freddie blew shrieks from an old bicycle horn that had lost its rubber squeezer. When we got to our favorite number, "Let's Make Some Noise," we ripped into the pots and pans cupboard and started banging away, letting that calypso beat blast the whole house.

Dad led a screaming conga line past the kitchen sink, picked up a dish towel, and snapped Mom's rear.

Now this is the sort of thing your mom might actually kind of like if your dad does it, but don't try it yourself. I did once and got a that'll-be-the-last-time-for-that look.

What my dad gets from her is pretend mad with a twinkle in her eye.

"Forget the dishes!" he said now. "We're celebrating!" He stuck the kazoo back in his mouth and grabbed her.

Then he broke away and put on the "William Tell Overture." In his stocking feet, he started running across the room and sliding on the wood floor. We'd chase after him, trying to get the hang of it.

He'd get a long slide going, then pretend to crash into the wall, arms and legs flying. *"Kerblam!"*

Mom was laughing, but she kept saying, "Be careful!" and shutting her eyes like she couldn't stand to look.

The babies thought Dad's stunts were great. By the time the music got to the thunderstorm part, we were all totally whipped up.

Then I slipped and hit the wall.

"Will you *please* take it easy?" Mom said. "I'd hate to be trying to explain this at the emergency room. 'Gee, officer, we were just teaching the kids how to slam into walls . . .' " She shook her head. "We'd get hauled in for child abuse so fast . . ."

Get hauled in . . . I stood up, shaky from more than the crash.

"Your mom's right," Dad said, winded. "We better calm down." He started peeling out of his flannel shirt. "I'm hot!"

"Hot!" Freddie said.

"Hot!" Lucy peeled out of her shirt. Her hair stood up in tufts.

Freddie's shirt got stuck on his head. He looked
like Lawrence of Arabia.

Mom made a face at Dad's T-shirt. "That should
have been in the rag bag six months ago."

Dad always wears his T-shirts until they have
these big holes in them. This one was definitely a
prime candidate for my favorite game.

"Mom?" I said with a hopeful look, glad to forget about police officers and school counselors.

Mom pretended to give this serious thought,
then she said our special signal words. "Sure
could use some new dust rags around here."

"Yippee!"

Right then the Lone Ranger part of the music
started. Dad took off. I followed.

"Now watch this," I shouted to the babies over
the music. "You gotta learn how we do this!"

Dad vaulted over the sofa and I scrambled after
him. He was still making noises on the kazoo, trying not to laugh, his eyes wide, his red cheeks
puffed out like a picture of the North Wind.

He started up the stairs but I hooked my hand
through a big hole in the back of his shirt and
yanked.

Lucy and Freddie shrieked.

Dad pretended to fall back down the stairs so
the babies could jump on him, too.

"That's right," I said, encouraging them. "Just
rip! It's okay!"

In about six seconds that T-shirt was nothing

but a neckband and sleeves with some ropey loops hanging from it.

Dad played beat for a minute while Freddie jumped up and down on his bare back. "Oof! Oof! Oof!" Then he rolled and escaped.

Laughing and shrieking, we took off after him. I was standing on the arm of the sofa, ready to leap off, when Mom yelled, "Quiet!"

The doorbell was ringing.

Dad looked at her. "Who in the heck . . . ?"

It's not like people just show up on your porch a lot out here in the woods.

Two bounces and I was down, heading for the door.

"Robby, no! Wait just a—"

Too late. I'd already flung it open. Standing on our front porch was Mrs. Van Gent and her husband, in spy-type trench coats!

"Well, hello there, Robby, I—" She stopped and stared at my shredded father.

The needle screeched across the record as Mom killed the Lone Ranger.

"Something tells me," Mrs. Van Gent said faintly, "there's been a little mix-up about our dinner."

Mortified. I'd heard that word. Now I didn't just know its meaning. I *felt* it. Dad's red face got three shades redder. For a moment I thought he might do what I felt like doing, which was run upstairs and pull a blanket over my head.

But he hardly missed a beat. He smiled at Mrs. Van Gent, caught his breath, and turned to me.

"Robby," he said. "Where are your manners? Find the lady a kazoo!"

□ 15 □

Bellyful of Trouble

"Now you've done it!" I yelled at Dad as soon as Mrs. Van Gent and her husband had scurried back to their car.

But Mom and Dad weren't paying any attention to me.

"I don't believe it." Mom sank onto the sofa. "I don't believe that just happened."

Dad had this dumb grin on his face.

Freddie of Arabia stood at the window yelling, "Good-bye, Yady. Good-bye, Yady . . ."

"I have *never*," Mom said, "in my whole life, been so embarrassed!"

But then she started laughing, excited-embarrassed more than mortified-embarrassed. She jumped up, shocked into action I guess, and started straightening the room. Which was totally dumb. It was way too late now.

Dad shook his head. "The look on that woman's face . . ."

"It's not funny!" I said.

"It's not?" Dad pulled off the tattered T-shirt. "Then how come we're laughing?"

"Because you don't understand. You guys don't know how serious this is. You have totally blown it, Dad!"

"*Me?* Hey sport, you helped with the shirt."

"I know, but you're the one that always gets things whipped up. I'm just a kid. I can't help it. You're the dad. You're supposed to be in charge!"

"Well, I am. I passed out the kazoos, didn't I?"

"Da-ad! Just think how this looked to her!"

"Hmmm." Dad rubbed his chin, squinting at me but talking to Mom. "Guess we're into that sensitive stage where any little thing we do will embarrass him."

I sucked in a deep breath and flung my arm to take in the whole pitiful scene. "You call this any little thing?"

"Hey, okay." Dad put his flannel shirt back on. "Take it easy. I'm sorry, all right?"

Lucy ran up to him with her fish puppet and started nipping at his leg. "Fishy fishy fishy!"

Mom crossed her arms over her chest and looked around the room. "We really can't blame him for being embarrassed."

"Guess not," Dad said. He snatched Lucy up, tossed her on the sofa, and gave her bare tummy a good tickle. She giggled and shrieked until he let her wriggle away. "But nobody ever died of embarrassment, Robby. In a week or two you'll have forgotten all about it."

"Are you kidding? I won't forget this if I live to be a hundred."

"Now don't be too hard on Dad," Mom said. "After all, it was your counselor who got the date wrong, not him."

I plopped on the sofa, thinking, *So what?* The point was, she *saw* us like this.

Then, out of the corner of my eye, I caught Lucy tiptoeing over to the door of Mom's studio. She turned the knob.

"Mo-om," I said in a warning voice.

Lucy pushed open the door.

"Hey!" Mom darted over and scooped Lucy up with one arm. "Bill? Did you see that? She opened the door."

Dad blinked. "That's what she did, all right."

"I mean, she opened the door by herself. It was shut tight."

Slowly, they both turned and looked at me.

Mom's voice was loaded with apologies. "Oh, Robby."

"I tried to tell you," I said, "but nobody ever believes me."

"I'm so sorry, Honey."

Yeah, great. Now I was so upset about everything else, I couldn't enjoy this apology one little
bit.

"I can't go to school," I told my parents Monday
morning. "I think I'm sick again."
"Do you suppose he's having a relapse of the
flu?" Mom put her hand on my forehead, TV-com-
mercial style.
"Could be," Dad said, studying my face. "Feel
like you're going to throw up?"
"No," I said quickly. "No, it's not that. My stomach just hurts."
I don't know why I felt like I was trying to get
away with something. I wasn't lying—my stomach
really did hurt.
Maybe it was because I knew perfectly well it
was Monday and Monday meant Mrs. Van Gent. I
did *not* want to have to face that lady.
Maybe it was because as soon as they said I
could stay home, my stomach felt better.

I had a lot of time to lie there and think that day
while I pretended to be sick, and here's what I
thought: You've heard about every cloud having a
silver lining? Well, the one good thing about this
disaster was that at least I could get my diorama
back.
Before, I had to stay on Mrs. Perkins's good side.
But what would it matter now? The damage was

done. I was sure Mrs. Van Gent had already told her what she'd seen at our house Friday night. By now the government probably had all the gory details too.

I might as well get the diorama for Dad. He could keep it as a memento of the great times we'd had before he blew it.

□ **16** □

Ambush!

When I showed up at school on Tuesday, I half expected everyone to be talking about my family being a bunch of jerks. But before I even got into the building, I found out we were not the big news.

Orin's dad was.

"Doctor says he's lucky he didn't get killed," Orin was bragging by the bike racks.

By noon recess, everybody in our class had heard about Elvis Downard's logging accident. Orin had thrilled us with the grisly details several times.

"That old fir just barber-chaired on him," he said, using his hands to show how the tree had snapped at a funny angle. "Dad says he shoulda knowed something bad was up. He couldn't sleep the night before, see, and his hands and feet were cold. Loggers all know that means trouble's ahead."

I have to admit, I was listening. Standing in the foursquare line, pretending to watch the game, I was actually running a little movie through my head: Accident on Douglas Mountain. In a weird way it sort of fascinated me to picture Elvis Downard gutting it out, the pain of that tree pinning his leg. I shivered. Pretty soon now Orin would get to the part where the leg bone was sticking through the skin . . .

Gee, I thought. I wish I had a dad worth bragging about. *Hey, guys, did you hear about the time my dad sliced his finger making guacamole? Blood? Oh lemme tell ya, we're talking two, maybe three Band-Aids . . .*

After break I went up to Mrs. Perkins's desk. She was counting up the Thanksgiving money we'd all turned in that morning. Mine was mostly from collecting returnable cans along the road.

"Mrs. Perkins, I've thought about it and I'm very sorry but I can't let you have my diorama for Mrs. Appleman because I want to give it to my dad."

She stopped counting. "Now hold on, Robert. When I asked you before . . ."

"You didn't really ask me, Mrs. Perkins. You *told* me. I didn't feel like I had any choice."

"But Robert, it's such an honor."

Right then Orin Downard swaggered in. Well, so

what if he overheard? Orin making fun of me was the least of my worries.

"I made the diorama especially for my dad, Mrs. Perkins, and it just wouldn't be right to give it to somebody else."

Yeah, I know, I wasn't making much sense. I was mad at Dad, right? But still . . .

"Ain't this touching," Orin said. "Got a hanky there, Darrel?" He faked a couple of sniffs. "Think I'm about to bust out bawling."

Mrs. Perkins slid the yellow envelope of money into her desk drawer. Then she looked up at me and shook her head.

"For-e-ver-more. Robert Hummer, you sure do take the cake."

I drew myself up. "Mrs. Perkins?" I said. "I really wish you'd call me Robby."

The wind rushed by my ears as I coasted down the road on my bike that afternoon, keeping far to the right to let the school bus pass. By the time I reached the first little bubbling creek that spills into the main creek, the sun had broken through the clouds, making sparklies of the raindrops on every twig and tree branch.

I was starting to feel a little less gloomy. At least I was getting away from the school. At least I was heading home.

And most important, I had the diorama in my back basket. No matter what else happened, this one thing was going to be the way I planned it. My dad was going to have the present I made for him.

And then, a rush of air as another bike swooped past. I swerved. When I'd steadied myself I saw it was Orin.

"Ya ya!" he yelled, pedaling away, holding something triumphantly over his head.

My diorama! He'd snagged it out of my back basket!

"Hey! You gimme that back!" I stood up to pedal, following him around the bend to the bridge. "Orin, come on! That's not funny!"

Through the dark tunnel of the bridge, I saw a figure silhouetted against the pale green light at the end.

Orin crossed ahead of me, threw down his bike, and tossed the boot box to the figure.

Bumpbumpbump. I pedaled furiously over the planks after them.

"Gimme a break, Orin." My voice echoed against the old timbers. "You're gonna wreck it."

"It's for his daddeee," Orin sing-songed, dancing around.

Out the other side, I jumped off my bike. The figure was Cody Riddle. He tossed the box back to Orin.

I shut my eyes. I could just imagine the little deer coming unglued, rattling against the sides, the sea gull on a thread banging crazily.

"Orin, please?" I hated the wimpy sound of my voice.

"Please?" he mimicked me.

I hated him. I wished I were bigger than him. I wished I could grab him and pound him. Having to beg Orin Downard for what was mine—it killed me!

"Okay," he said, "here it is!"

But instead of tossing it to me, Orin hauled off and sent the box in a flying arc over the creek.

"No!" I watched it splash into the gurgling water.

I scrambled down the bank, sliding through the wet ferns, keeping my eye on the box as it floated like a little ark, twirling in the eddies and bumping against a mossy rock, the rush of water holding it there for an instant.

I waded into the iciness up to my knees and fished it out. Standing on a rock at the edge, I held it up to the light and peeked through the eyehole.

That was Nekomah Creek all right. Nekomah Creek after an end-of-the-world flood. All the paint had run, the parts made of tissue looked like wet toilet paper. I tried the battery-powered lights —shorted out.

Above me at the bridge, Orin and Cody were laughing their heads off.

Hot tears sprang to my eyes. My throat ached. This is where I should have raised my fist and yelled *I'll get you for this, Orin Downard. I'll get you for this if it's the last thing I do!* That's how it would have gone in a movie or a book.

But this was stupid, crummy, real life. So I just hugged the ruined box to me, climbed the slippery bank, and got on my bike.

"Hurry on home," Orin sang after me in his nastiest voice. "Hurry up and tattle to that big tough daddy of yours!"

They didn't chase me, but I could hear their stupid laughing at my back all the way down the road.

□ 17 □

Pumpkins Every Time

I shoved open our front door.

"I hate Orin Downard!" I shouted. "I hate hate hate him!"

Mom came out of her studio. "Honey, what's wrong?" She took a closer look. "Robby, your feet are all wet. You're all muddy."

"Just look at this!" I flung down the soggy remains of my diorama and told her what Orin had done.

"Oh, dear." She stooped and picked it up.

"And I was going to give it to Dad for his birthday."

"Well . . ." She peeked through the eyehole. "Maybe we can fix it."

"No, it's ruined. It's just totally ruined." I swallowed hard. "And it was really neat, too. Even

Mrs. Perkins said it was the best one in the school."

"I'm sure it was wonderful." She held it up to the light. "I can tell that even now." Then she set it down and let out a big disgusted sigh. "What is the *matter* with that kid, anyway?"

"He just hates me. And I don't even know why."

She looked out the leaded windows in the direction of the Downards' place. "Maybe today he was upset about his dad's accident." She turned back to me. "You heard, didn't you?"

"Yeah, everybody did. How'd you find out?"

"Oh, you know how fast news like that gets around Nekomah Creek. So. Orin took it pretty hard?"

"Oh, Mom, are you kidding? Orin *loved* it— bragged and spouted logger talk all day. No, he just wrecked my project for the fun of it, that's all."

"Now, now . . ."

"And I'm going to get him for this, Mom. I'd like to beat him up."

"But Robby, what good would that do? It wouldn't fix your diorama."

"I know, but it'd make me feel better."

"Think so, huh?"

I nodded stubbornly. Then I realized something funny was going on. Mom and I were talking and nobody was interrupting.

I looked around. "Where is everybody?"

"The kids never did settle down for much of a nap, and since I'd be here when you got home, Dad thought he'd take them to the library and then grocery shopping."

"Oh." I'd been so upset, I hadn't even noticed the minivan was gone.

"Now let's get these wet shoes off you. Sit down by the fire here and I'll fix you some hot chocolate. When you're warmed up we can drive in to The Palette for supplies to make a new diorama."

"Start it all over?" I let out a big sigh. "I just couldn't."

"Start something else, then. Come on, how about it?"

Usually a trip to the art store perks me right up, but not today.

It was dark and raining hard by the time we chugged our way home around Tillicum Head.

Mom glanced at me. "Think maybe you've still got a touch of the flu?"

I shook my head.

"You feel okay, then?"

I shrugged.

We drove a little farther. Weird, having Mom to myself—no sounds but the rumbling engine and the squeak of the windshield wipers. I took a sideways peek at her face, faintly lit by the dashboard lights. Now that I had a chance to talk, I couldn't bring myself to mention what was really bugging me. Instead I tried to edge in around it.

"Mom?"

"Hm?" She kept her eyes on the curvy, rain-slick road.

"This is really dumb, but sometimes I feel two different ways about one thing." I was thinking how I half admired Elvis Downard and half hated him. How I sort of liked Mrs. Van Gent but was scared of her too. How I loved the way Dad acted but also felt embarrassed by him. "Do you know what I mean?"

"Sure. That's what grown-ups call having mixed feelings."

"Oh." Mixed feelings. So there was an official name for this? Part of me was relieved. Maybe I was normal. On the other hand, if it was normal to be confused, did that mean I'd feel this way forever? I watched the string of orange reflectors snaking toward us along the center of the road. Oh, great! Now I was having mixed feelings about mixed feelings!

"Well, one thing I know for sure," I said. "I'd still like to beat up Orin Downard."

"Robby—"

"And I wish Dad could beat up Elvis."

Mom sighed.

"Well, Orin's always bugging me about that. I never want to tell Dad this, but Orin's always saying, 'Nyeah nyeah, your dad's a wimp. My dad could pound your dad any day.' "

"That is *so* silly."

"I know, but . . . I can't help it, Mom! Sometimes I wish I had the kind of dad who would be bigger and tougher than all the other dads."

She glanced at me. "Robby, this isn't the stone age. We don't rate fathers on which one can beat up the others. What do we need with that? Wouldn't you rather just have a dad who loves you, a dad who's a lot of fun?"

"But Mom, you always act like Dad wants to have *too* much fun."

"Oh, I know . . ." She laughed. "But really, is there ever such a thing as too much fun?"

There is if your counselor sees it, I thought darkly.

"I'm sure your dad's right with all his talk about priorities. You kids will remember those pumpkins all your lives. You won't care that the shed was always a mess."

"But you care."

"Well, there you go—mixed feelings! But actually—and this might surprise you—if you gave me a choice, I'd go for those pumpkins every time."

"You would?"

"Of course! And believe me, Robby, I've seen a lot of dads. They don't come any better than yours."

My throat got tight. Good thing it was dark and

Mom couldn't see my face. Sure, deep down I thought Dad was the greatest. But who cared about my opinion? Not Mrs. Van Gent, not Mrs. Perkins, not the government.

I stared at the zaps of rain shooting straight at the windshield through the headlights.

Up Nekomah Creek Road, we passed the Downards' place. All dark. Probably they were at the hospital.

Then we turned between the two big fir trees and there was our house. Usually I loved the way it looked on a rainy night, lit from inside, each window a rectangle of gold. Best of all were the colored jewels in the stained-glass half-circle over my loft. But tonight it almost made me feel bad somehow. I stepped down into the crunchy gravel, taking in the smell of wood smoke, the faint sound of Zydeco music blasting away inside. In the window, the faces of two happy little werewolves pressed against the glass, waiting for us.

Our home on the banks of Nekomah Creek. Orin ruining my model of it was bad enough, but that was nothing compared to worrying about losing the real thing.

□ **18** □

A Beautiful Day in the Neighborhood

When I got home from school the next day, I dropped my backpack on the kitchen floor and stared at Dad. "You're going to *what*?"

"Shh! The kids are still asleep."

"Oh, sorry, but—"

"I said I'm taking the Downards a casserole."

"But why?"

"Because we heard they brought Elvis home from the hospital this morning and it's the neighborly thing to do."

"Dad! The Downards are our enemies!"

"Robby, we don't want enemies. We didn't move up here to fight with people. We wanted to live in a small community where neighbors still helped each other like in the old days."

"But you don't *like* them," I accused him. "Don't

you remember after those hearings you went to? You said Elvis Downard's ancestors were probably the ones who first started killing off all the buffalo and that their family hadn't changed since. You said Douglas Mountain would be nothing but stumps if they had their way."

Dad sighed. "I know I said that, Robby. And I still think it's probably true. But the Downards are in trouble, and trouble has a way of putting things in perspective."

I frowned. "What's that mean?"

"Well, in your drawings you make something that's farther away smaller, right? It's like that. It's seeing which things are big and important and up close and which things ought to be smaller and in the background. Right now I'm putting Elvis Downard's broken bones up closer than his politics."

"Okay, but even forgetting politics, it's only been twenty-four hours since Orin tossed my diorama in the creek. At school he teased me about it all day long. And now you're going to reward his family by being nice?"

"It's not a reward. It's got nothing to do with anything they've done or not done." He put foil over the casserole and tucked it into a grocery bag. "I just wouldn't feel right, that's all, pretending we hadn't heard about his father's accident."

"Okay," I said, "but do you have to take"—I made a face—"*food?*"

"What's wrong with food? When people are in trouble, they sometimes don't have time to cook. Or they forget to. But they need to eat to keep up their strength."

"Yeah, but . . . Dad? I didn't want to tell you this, but . . . well, their whole family thinks it's weird that you cook."

/ Dad smiled. "Oh, do they?"

"Yes, and it's not funny! Orin says it's disgusting and not normal that you stay home and Mom goes to work. He's always saying his dad can pound you."

"Oh. So that's it."

I nodded.

"Well, even if he feels that way, Robby, the man is completely laid up. He's in no condition to . . . to *pound* me."

"Okay, so he's probably not going to punch you out over a casserole. But what if they laugh?"

"Laugh?"

"Yeah! What if they laugh at you?"

"Then I'll laugh too, and we'll all have a good yuk. Hey, should I take my kazoo? That might cheer him up!" He pulled a kazoo out of his shirt pocket, stuck it in his mouth, and started humming Mr. Rogers's "Won't You Be My Neighbor" song.

I blew a slow stream of air up at my forehead. How could I tell him I was just plain tired of people thinking of me as the son of a nut?

"Dad, could you be serious for once?"

He stopped. He tossed the kazoo on the counter and sighed. "Okay, Robby. Here's how it is. I don't like the idea of going over there any better than you do. Actually, I dread it. I will be *extremely* glad to have it over with. I know how they feel about us. But you can't always take the easy route. That saying—'a man's gotta do what a man's gotta do'—it isn't just a joke. You have to do what you know is right whether you like it or not, that's all. And who knows? Maybe something good'll come out of it."

"Huh. Like what?"

"I don't know, Robby, but if I don't do this, it's going to keep bugging me that I should have." He pulled on his stocking hat.

"But, Dad!" I was so glad I thought of this. "The babies! You can't go off and leave them alone!"

"Nice try," Dad said, "but Mom's working in her studio with the intercom turned on. She'll hear them when they wake up. Now, are you coming with me or not?"

Well, I couldn't let him do it alone, could I?

A light mist was falling as we walked out over our plank bridge. Dad carried the casserole and I hugged a loaf of homemade bread to my chest like it was a teddy bear I needed for courage.

As we passed our mailbox Dad turned to me. "Now what were you telling me about the Thanksgiving money?"

"Oh, yeah." I'd come home with big news but

forgot all about it when I found Dad packing food for the Downards. "Well," I began again, "somebody stole the money we collected right out of Mrs. Perkins's desk."

"That's too bad."

"Yeah. Just think of all those pop cans we collected."

"And they don't have any idea who did it?"

"Guess not. I thought maybe it was Orin, but then Mrs. Perkins said it was taken right after school yesterday, and that's when he was down by the bridge, wrecking my diorama."

"Even Orin can't be everywhere, doing every bad thing at once, huh?"

"Right." I shifted the bread. "I tried to find out some other evidence, like if anything else was missing from her desk, but Mrs. Perkins just goes, 'Robby, this is not an Encyclopedia Brown case. If you know anything about it, tell us. Otherwise, it's none of your business.'" I scowled. "I don't like her very much."

"I get that idea."

"And she doesn't like me either." I waited for him to deny this.

"Well, that's the way it goes sometimes."

I blinked, surprised.

"You're not going to hit it off with every teacher the way you did with Mrs. Kassel last year."

Real comforting. Well, at least he was honest.

We had reached the Downards' mailbox now.

Over it hung a shingle that said "Dressmaking." It seemed strange, walking right up the driveway I'd hurried past so many times before. When the dogs spotted us they started barking and jerking against their chains.

I looked at Dad. Maybe he'd decide to turn back?

But he gave the dogs a few pats and they calmed down, sniffing us in a friendly way as we went up the front steps.

Dad knocked on the door.

I heard some yelling inside, then the door swung back.

Orin. His eyes got as big as beady little ground-hog eyes can get. He looked nervous. Maybe he thought I'd brought Dad over to get him in trouble about the diorama.

"Hi, Orin," Dad said. "We thought we'd look in on your dad. Is he up for visitors?"

Orin checked out Dad's brown bag covered casserole. "What's that?" he said, like he thought maybe we were delivering a bomb.

"This," Dad said, "is chicken à la Hummer."

Orin's mom appeared behind him. "Orin, if we have company, don't make them—" Then she saw us. "Oh," she said. "Oh, hello."

I'd seen Mrs. Downard at school programs. She always seemed too thin and delicate to be Orin's mom. Today she looked pretty tired.

"We were sorry to hear about your husband's

accident," Dad said. "We just brought a couple of things to help out with your meals."

"Oh. Well, that's real nice." The lines between her eyebrows smoothed out. "Come on in. Elvis is just watching some TV."

I glanced at Dad, hoping we could drop the food and go, but he walked right in like he always visited the homes of people who hated him.

Off to the left I caught a glimpse of Mrs. Downard's sewing room—fabric piled everywhere, a couple of frilly dresses hanging on a rack. Sometimes at night we'd be driving by and we'd see her working in here, framed in the lit-up window, bent over her sewing machine.

"Now don't be looking in there," she said, hurrying to close the door. "Such a mess." We followed her into the living room.

Was it stuffy in here or was it me? I couldn't breathe. I stood with my arms tight to my sides so I wouldn't knock off any of the little figurines that were on every shelf and table. And the walls! I'd never seen so many pictures before. Orin's mom really had their place decorated fancy.

Elvis sprawled on the sofa with his eyes closed, his broken arm in a sling, his leg cast propped on a coffee table made out of a thick disk of tree trunk, sanded and varnished. A game of checkers was on the table too.

"Elvis, Honey? Bill Hummer and his boy are here."

Elvis grunted. It wasn't friendly. On the other hand, I could see he wasn't about to jump up and slug Dad, either. He glanced at us and nodded. He ran a hand through his messy hair and turned back to the giant-screen TV.

"He's not himself," Mrs. Downard whispered. "Still having a lot of pain."

Not himself was right. He looked so different from the way he had in class the other day. His face was kind of gray and creased. He seemed smaller.

"They brought a nice casserole and some home-made bread," Mrs. Downard said. "Wasn't that thoughtful?"

Elvis grunted again, one point higher on a scale from mean to friendly.

Dad started the small talk—how we'd heard about the accident. How we were real sorry about it but were glad it wasn't worse and all that. How we'd be glad to help them out any way we could.

I noticed a bunch of get-well cards on the mantel. One was one of my mother's designs! After the first surprise, my muscles loosened a little. Funny —just knowing that a friend of the Downards liked my mom's artwork made me feel better about the Downards themselves.

Orin watched us, head hunched into his shoulders. He looked different today too. Almost timid. His little sister Peggy came down the hall, dragging her hand along the wall. She sidled over and tucked her head under her mother's arm.

I had the feeling Elvis just wished we'd leave. He never even turned the TV down the whole time Dad tried to make conversation.

Finally, without taking his eyes off the screen, he said, "Sherilyn?"

"Yes, Elvis?" Orin's mom hurried over to him.

"How 'bout another one of them pills?"

"Oh, dear. Hurtin' pretty bad, is it?" She glanced at their cuckoo clock. "Still another hour before the next one. The doctor said—"

"Forget the doctor!" Elvis's good arm jerked like he wanted to hit the guy in charge of the pills. "Just gimme one."

She jumped to get it.

Boy, my dad would never talk to my mom that way, no matter what kind of shape he was in. And if he did my mom would probably just go, "What's with *you* today, Buster?"

"Well," Dad said. "We didn't mean to tire you out." He turned to Mrs. Downard. "That's a big pile of rounds you've got out there. Could I split some of that up for you? I've got some time here before I need to get dinner on."

She glanced at Elvis. "Gee, that'd be—"

"Naw! I'll do it," Elvis said.

Dad tried to kid him about it. "Come on, now, Elvis. It's going to be a while before you're up to that."

Elvis grunted, partly like he had to agree, partly like he was hurting.

Well, I never thought I'd be saying this about Elvis Downard, but I felt sorry for him. Being big and strong is great, but big and strong can be gone as fast as a Doug fir can crack the wrong way.

"Well, thanks then," Elvis said. "I guess I'll have to owe you."

"Don't worry about it," Dad said.

Orin's mom looked pleased. I think she hadn't liked Dad before, but now she did.

"Get your jacket on, Orin," she said. "You two kids can help him stack it."

"But Mo-om . . ."

"Git!" Elvis snapped, his good arm jerking again.

The air outside felt cool and soft on my face. We had gone in there and we had survived.

Orin came down the steps, pulling on his parka. He glanced at me, then looked away.

Together we watched my dad take his jacket off and roll up the sleeves of his flannel shirt. He made a big show of spitting on his palms, then rubbing them together. He winked at me. Then he spread his legs, hoisted the ax, and started splitting those logs.

Now I have some favorite sounds, like the sound of the babies giggling. That's a tough one to beat. But there's not much that's nicer than the ring of an ax in the stillness as a pile of firewood's getting split.

Right then, standing there with Orin, both of us watching my dad swinging that ax, I felt kind of proud. Who cared what anyone else thought? *I* thought my dad was one heck of a guy.

I looked at Orin and hoped he knew what I was thinking. I was thinking, yeah, that's right, that's my dad. He can chop wood *and* he can make a casserole.

□ 19 □

A Kid's Gotta Do What a Kid's Gotta Do

As soon as we started home, I thought Dad would say, "There. Now that wasn't so bad, was it?"

But he didn't say anything. He just turned up his jacket collar against the mist and began whistling.

I fell in step beside him and wondered: Did I feel better now because we'd done the right thing? Or did I just feel better because the visit was over?

"Hey, Robby!"

I turned around. It was Orin, standing at the end of his driveway.

"Can I talk to you?" he called.

I looked at Dad to see what I should do, but he just shrugged. Then he checked his watch. "I've got to get dinner going."

I looked at Orin again. "Okay," I told Dad. "I'll be home in a minute."

Dad headed up the road. I turned and slowly walked back toward Orin.

He picked up a pebble and threw it into the ditch. Then he threw another one. Finally he said, "I know who stole the Thanksgiving money."

"You do? Who?"

"Nathan Steckler."

"Oh." I believed it. Nathan was mean enough. Then I remembered something. "Wait a minute—isn't Nathan's dad one of the guys laid off at the mill? That's who the money was supposed to help in the first place."

Orin shrugged.

Weird. Well, maybe this was what Mrs. Van Gent meant when she talked about stress in families where the dad's unemployed.

"The thing is," Orin went on, "the teachers think I did it."

"You couldn't of," I said. "You were . . . you weren't at the school when it happened."

"Yeah." Orin's face went pink. He couldn't look me in the eye, remembering about my diorama. "But they caught me with this water pistol, see. It was in Mrs. Perkins's desk and Nathan must've swiped it along with the money. Then he gave it to me."

"But Cody knows you weren't at the school."

"Huh. Cody's on Nathan's side. He told them Nathan was at the bridge with him."

"But that's a lie!"

Orin snorted. "Great pals, huh?" He threw another rock. "Looks like you're the only one who
knows *I* was at the bridge."

"Yeah, so?"

"So will you tell them?"

I frowned. "It would just be my word against
Cody's."

"Yeah, but Robby . . ." Orin looked at me.
"Your word . . ." He shook his head. "I mean, the
teachers would believe you."

I blinked. Would they?

Orin looked at his feet. " 'Course I couldn't
blame you for not sticking up for me. Not after
what I did . . ."

His words hung there. I waited for him to come
out with it, say he was sorry about my diorama.
Then it hit me—this was as close to an apology as
Orin knew how to give.

"The thing is, if they call my dad in and tell him
I took that money . . ." He sucked in his breath
and opened his eyes real wide, like he needed to
blink off tears. "He'll whip my butt."

I thought about that. Orin deserved it, maybe
not for this, but for every other crummy thing he'd
done. I'd been wanting to whip him myself, right?
But somehow . . . well, when I pictured his dad
actually doing it, I just got this sick feeling in my
stomach.

"So could you— Come on, Robby, will you tell
them the truth?" He looked right at me. "Please?"

Funny, for a moment there he reminded me of Freddie when he was watching me fix his Buddy Wabbit. So hopeful, so kind of desperate, like he was really depending on me.

I glanced back up the road. Dad had disappeared around the bend. I still didn't trust Orin any farther than I could throw him. I'm not stupid. I could get him out of this pickle and he might be making my life miserable again the very next day.

But maybe that didn't matter. The truth was the truth. Like Dad says, a man's gotta do what a man's gotta do.

I guess a kid does too.

"I'll tell them," I said. "I'll tell them you were at the bridge with me."

Now I won't try to convince you Orin and I became best buddies because of this. I'd be surprised if we ever get to be friends at all. But he did quit giving me a hard time at school, and since the day I stuck up for him in the principal's office, he has never said one bad thing about my dad.

□ 20 □

One Last Chance

"Notice anything different?" Rose asked me before school Friday morning.

"About you?"

"Yeah. Something new."

I finished locking my bike to the stand, stood up, and checked her over.

"Oh. New shoes, huh?"

She nodded, lit up like she was standing there in her own personal sunbeam instead of the gray morning mist. "And that's not all. I've even got some money for books. You know, for Powell's tomorrow."

"Oh. Yeah. That's great." I didn't have the heart to tell her the trip to Powell's might not happen.

Actually, I was having a hard time picturing to-

morrow at all. I was too worried about Dad's gourmet dinner for Mrs. Van Gent tonight.

Now it's easy enough to say, *Oh who gives a rip
what other people think, I know my dad is great.*
But let's face it—my opinion was not the only one
that mattered. This dinner had to be perfect.

"Robby, what's the matter?"

"Oh, nothing."

"You look . . . sad. Aren't you excited about
tomorrow?"

"Sure." I sighed, thinking. Could I trust her with
this? "Rose, you know about Amber Hixon getting
sent to a foster home? And your mom thinks it's so
unfair?"

"Well . . . did I say that?"

I looked at her. "Yes, don't you remember? You
said your mom told you the government took kids
just because they didn't like the way people
lived."

"Yeah . . ." Her eyes slid away from mine. "But
she sort of changed her mind about that. After all,
we haven't been here that long. She didn't really
know the Hixons. When she heard the stories
about them, she said the social workers probably
did the right thing."

"What stories?"

Rose lowered her voice so the kids walking by
wouldn't hear. "Mrs. Lukes says they used to ask
her to baby-sit for a couple hours and then they

wouldn't come back for days. One time they'd gone all the way to Las Vegas!"

"You're kidding."

"No, really. After a while they quit doing that but it turned out they were just leaving Amber all by herself. All night!"

"Wow. They shouldn't do that."

"I know, but they did."

"It doesn't make sense, though. Why would parents nice enough to buy a kid a pony be so mean in other ways?"

"Oh, Robby, Amber doesn't have a pony."

I looked at her. I thought about the toy pony with the rhinestone bridle. "I guess not."

"One of my sister's friends lives next to them. She says Amber makes up all kinds of stories."

Hard to know what to believe, hard to imagine someone lying so easily. That string of fibs I'd told Mrs. Van Gent had knotted my stomach like a pretzel.

"Wouldn't you feel kind of sick inside," I said, "if you told lies all the time like that?"

Rose thought for a moment. "Maybe she doesn't think of them as lies. Maybe to her they're more like wishes."

I looked up at the ridgeline, a jag of treetops sticking out of the fog. I guess my situation and Amber's weren't as alike as I'd thought.

"Or maybe she *did* feel sick inside," I said.

Rose stooped to rub a smudge off one of her new

shoes. "Did I tell you we saw her at the Douglas Bay Safeway?"

"Yeah? How did she look?"

"Fine, really. She was pushing a shopping cart for this lady—I think maybe it was her new foster mother."

"And she didn't look miserable?"

"No. At least she didn't throw herself at our feet going 'Save me! Save me!' or anything. She said hi friendly enough." Rose stood and glanced toward the school building. We were the last kids left outside. "And also, about my mom . . . well, it was a social worker in Douglas Bay who finally tracked down my dad. Now we should be getting money from him, regular. The first check just came. That's how I got new shoes. And book money." She smiled—almost an apology. "So you can see how my mom wouldn't be so down on social workers anymore."

I nodded. I was having trouble taking all this in.

"Come on. We'll be late." Rose reached the door ahead of me, pulled it open, and looked back. "Are you *sure* Amber wasn't your girlfriend?"

All I could think about all day was the dinner, even while I played soccer at recess. One thing I'll say for sports, when you're too worried to make sense out of the words on a page, you can still run up and down a field. So all the time I was chasing the ball, trying for a good, satisfying kick, I was worrying about whether or not Dad was right this minute cleaning the house like he was supposed to.

Because even if social workers did help people who really needed it, I still didn't see how they could be anything but a hassle for us Hummers if they got the wrong idea.

After school I pedaled home as fast as I could and shoved open the front door.

"Wobby! Hi, Wobby!"

I sagged against the doorjamb. A scene straight out of my nightmares—the house a world-class wreck, Freddie and Lucy still going strong.

"Dad!" I dropped my backpack and ran across to the kitchen. "Did you forget? The gourmet dinner's tonight!"

"Hi, Robby." He was whistling while he cut up vegetables. "No, I didn't forget."

"But the *house*, Dad. You were gonna clean it all up."

"It's not too bad, is it?" He went to the edge of the big main room and blinked like somebody just waking up.

Oh, for Pete's sake! Why waste time even talking to him? I dropped to the floor and started tossing toys into the wicker basket.

Freddie and Lucy started tossing them out.

"Come on, you guys. Please don't." If only they understood how serious this was.

Then I heard the truck on the gravel. I ran out onto the porch.

"Mom! Quick! You've got to help!"

She slammed the truck door and rushed up the steps, her face white. "What? Tell me! Is somebody hurt?"

"No, no, everyone's fine. It's the house, Mom. It's a wreck!"

She braced herself on the doorjamb, hand over her heart. "Robby, don't you ever scare me like that again."

"Sorry," I said, more miserable than ever.

But then after a deep breath, she walked in and looked around. "Oh, my gosh!" She slapped a hand over her face, then peeked out between spread fingers, maybe hoping she'd got it wrong on the first glance. Nope. Pit City. "Bill!" She aimed herself toward the kitchen.

"Hi, Honey." Dad wiped his hands on a dish towel, all smiles.

"It's about this"—Mom pointed, sharp and accusing—"this . . . trash heap we call our home."

Dad's smile got guiltier. He shrugged. "Not much use picking it up until we get the kids out of here, is there?"

She glanced away, then turned back. "Darn it, Bill! This is supposed to be your dinner. You're going to be busy cooking. You know very well who that leaves to straighten all this up. Yours truly."

Dad looked offended. "Is that so unfair? I can't do everything around here by myself, can I?"

Mom sucked in her breath. "Of course not. Not when you're always so busy being Mr. Fun."

"Huh?"

Mom glared at him. "Didn't you ever stop to think that I might be a lot more fun myself if I wasn't always having to clean up after *your* fun?" She yanked her jacket zipper down. "You *promised* to do this and you've been putting it off for days. Every time I mentioned it you acted like, oh, don't be a nag."

I threw myself on the sofa and pulled a pillow over my head. This was great. Not only would Mrs. Van Gent see our house messy, she'd also find my folks yelling at each other.

"Now wait a minute," Dad said. "I never called you a nag."

"Well, you rolled your eyes. You made me feel like one."

"Hey, I can't be responsible for the way you interpret my eyeballs every time they twitch!"

"I must have been out of my mind," Mom said, "trusting you'd have this place shoveled out by the time I got home." She pulled her jacket zipper back up. "I have half a mind to just walk out and let you stew in your own juice!"

I pulled away my pillow and rolled off the sofa at Mom's feet. "No, Mom, don't!"

"Don't worry, Robby. Mom's not going anywhere." Dad aimed his best apologizing smile at her.

Mom wasn't having any of it. "Don't you *dare* try to cute your way out of this."

"Oh look, the food'll be so good nobody'll even notice what the—"

"And don't give me that either! Anyone with eyes can see this is a pigpen! Maybe I should just bundle up the kids and take them all to Burger King."

"No, Mom, you can't. Please!" I was on my knees now. "It was so awful last week when Mrs. Van Gent came. If she finds the house like this again, and then if she gets the idea you're not here because you guys are fighting . . ."

Mom and Dad turned from each other and stared at me.

"Robby, what is it?" Dad said.

Concerned Looks! For once I was glad.

Mom pulled me up. "Honey, try to calm down."

"I can't." I was ready to cry. "I can't because— you guys just don't understand. This is our last chance. If you can't show that counselor we've got a good home, they might—" My dumb voice trailed off to a squeak . . . I gulped hard. "They might ship us kids off to some stupid foster home!"

"What kids?" Dad said.

"Us! Me and Lucy and Freddie!" Then it all came pouring out. About Amber being put in a foster home, about me worrying the counselor thought our family was strange. How Dad had been doing such a super job of proving it.

"And Mom," I said, "remember when we were goofing off right before Mrs. Van Gent showed up last week? You said yourself about police officers at the emergency room and all that."

"Oh, Honey, I was just kidding. I didn't mean to scare you."

"And what about that stuff on TV, Dad? All those people trying to get their kids back?"

"But that hasn't got anything to do with you."

"Well, it might if we're not careful. I don't want to be sitting in some stranger's house, watching you and Mom on TV crying to all those government people about losing us."

Dad and Mom gave each other sad, guilty looks. This sure had put a lid on the house-cleaning fight.

"Robby," Dad said, "I don't know why those people lost their kids, but I *do* know that's not going to happen to you."

I sniffed. "Are you sure?"

"Yeah, I'm sure. This is a happy family, isn't it? Aren't you happy?"

"Well, I was. Before all this."

"When kids get sent to foster homes, it's because their parents aren't taking care of them. We take care of you, don't we?"

I nodded.

"We're talking about parents who may even be beating up on their kids."

I cringed. I didn't even want to think about that.

"You know," Mom said, "Amber's parents must have been incredibly young when they got married. They're still just like kids themselves."

"Maybe if they do some growing up," Dad said, "she can come back. In the meantime, she's probably better off with someone else."

"But Dad, that's just how *you* are. Even Mom's always saying you're just like a kid."

"Oh, but Honey, that's different," Mom said. "It's okay to be like a kid when it comes to having fun."

"It is?"

"Sure. Just as long as you act grown up about the grown-up stuff. See what I mean?"

"I guess so." I wiped my hand across my eyes to catch a couple of tears that had sneaked out. "But you know what? I was so scared when I talked to the counselor that . . . well, I lied. I told her Dad was getting a job. They don't like it when dads are unemployed."

"Oh, Robby," Dad said, "I think you misunderstood. They're just hoping all the families have enough money to take care of their kids right. They probably don't realize I'm staying home for a couple of years because I want to."

"Well, I tried to tell Mrs. Van Gent that, but she doesn't believe me."

"I'd be glad to talk to her, if it'll make you feel better."

I nodded, and right then I had kind of a weird, guilty thought. "You know what, Dad? Sometimes I kinda wish you *did* go off to a job. Just to be like other dads."

"Well, I'll probably go back to teaching in a couple of years."

"The thing is, Robby," Mom said, "this is such a precious time for us, having you kids. We don't want to miss it. We don't want to be working so hard at our jobs that we wake up one morning and say, 'Hey, what happened? They all grew up on us!' "

"That's right," Dad said. "I won't get another chance to be a daddy. That's the main thing I don't want to blow. Even if we do go into debt."

"What do you mean, go into debt?" Mom said. "We're going to make a fortune in greeting cards!"

"Right!" Dad said. "So. Robby, are we clear on this? That you don't have to worry about being taken away?"

"Well . . . if you say so." I let out a huge sigh. Then I looked around the room again. "But Dad? Even if she isn't going to ship me to a foster home, could we still try to make things nice for Mrs. Van Gent, just so that, you know, we won't feel so . . . embarrassed?"

"I'm all for that," Mom said. But she didn't seem mad at Dad anymore. "Come on, I'll drive you kids over to Mrs. Lukes's and your dad and I'll get to work."

"No way," I said. "I'm staying right here. You guys need all the help you can get."

"So what are we waiting for?" Dad said. As Mom herded the little guys toward the door, he put on the zippiest record we have and started throwing pillows here, tossing toys there. I pitched in at breakneck speed, filling a wastebasket with half-eaten snacks and trashed junk mail.

Zydeco housekeeping!

□ 21 □

The Fancy Romancey Dinner

Well, Dad was right about the kerosene lamps. In the soft glow that lit the room, Mrs. Van Gent would never notice that he'd decided to skip dusting in favor of giving me table-waiting lessons. And she'd never guess that behind every closet door was an avalanche of stuff waiting to bury anybody thinking to be tidy and hang up their coat.

Or anybody thinking to spy.

Right on the dot of seven the doorbell rang.

I hung back while Mom opened the door. Mrs. Van Gent was standing there in her trench coat, her husband beside her. I saw her eyes flick past Mom, a quick once-over of the house.

"Mrs. Van Gent," Mom said. "Come on in."

"Oh, please, call me Heidi."

Heidi? Whoever heard of a spy named Heidi?

"Well," she said, stepping inside. She looked relieved. "This is my husband, Steve."

Mom nodded at him. "Dr. Van Gent." He was a dentist, see.

"No, Heidi's right. Make it Steve." He smiled. Big white flashing teeth. Probably helped him get patients.

Dad came out and we all got introduced to each other.

"Here, let me take those." Mom helped them get out of their coats. She headed for the closet.

"I'll do it!" I grabbed the coats and detoured to the hall tree. *Whew.* Guess Mom forgot we were on avalanche alert.

Mrs. Van Gent—er, Heidi—shook out her hair. Good grief! It went all the way to her waist. She was wearing a thick white sweater and jeans tucked into tall boots—a lot more relaxed looking than at school.

"Your house is gorgeous!" she said.

I glanced at Dad. He winked.

"I just love what you've done with the recycled wood." She turned to her husband. "Wouldn't it be fun to redo your waiting room like this? The Country Look is so popular now."

The Country Look? I thought this was the Picked-Up Look.

"Well, we like it," Dad said. "It's home."

"It's a *great* home," I said to Mrs. Van Gent,
hoping she'd know I wasn't just talking woodwork
and stained glass.

She nodded without looking at me. "Are the
twins here?"

"If the twins were here," I said, "believe me,
you'd know it."

"Oh, too bad." She smiled at Mom and Dad.
"I've heard so much about them, I was really looking forward to seeing them."

"Well," Dad said, "I don't think we'd have a
prayer of pulling off a nice dinner with them
around."

They all laughed these funny little heh-heh
laughs. Then it was quiet. Dr. Van Gent coughed.

Dad went into his headwaiter act. "Table for two?"

Heh heh. They all looked like they felt silly, pretending this was a restaurant. Dad pulled out a chair for Mrs. Van Gent and seated her at the table he'd set up in front of the wood stove.

"Isn't this nice?" she said, but watching from the kitchen, I thought she seemed stiff. No wonder. She and her husband couldn't really talk like in a real restaurant, not with us hearing every word.

Next Dad sent me in with a bottle of wine and a dish towel hung over my arm like he'd showed me.

"From the Nehalem Winery," I said in my snootiest voice. "Nineteen eighty-eight. A very good year."

"Sounds fine." Dr. Van Gent smiled. Those teeth!

Dad had already loosened the cork for me, so I took it off and poured a little in a glass.

"Really the waiter's supposed to drink this," I said, "to make sure you don't swallow any little cork gunkies. But Dad told me not to." I fixed a meaningful look on Mrs. Van Gent. "My dad would never, ever let any kids drink wine."

"I'm sure he wouldn't, Robby."

"I just wanted you to know. I wanted to make sure you understood that my folks take good care of me."

Now she really looked puzzled. "Well, of course they do."

Dad hustled in from the kitchen. "So." He clapped his hands together and looked from Mrs. Van Gent to her husband. "How's it going?"

"Oh, fine, fine," they both said.

"Fine," Dad said.

"I'm just getting ready to pour the wine," I told him. "This is the glass with cork gunkies."

"Oh, well, I'll take care of that." Dad picked up the glass and drank. "Say, I've tasted some cork gunkies in my time, but these are truly outstanding!"

"Da-ad!" I poured wine in the other two glasses. "You're supposed to sniff it," I told Dr. Van Gent.

"Whatever you say." He sniffed. "Smells okay to me."

Pretty clear this guy didn't take his wine too seriously. I glanced at Dad. That was fine with him.

He passed his own glass under his nose and breathed deep. "Ah! Such a wonderful bouquet. Playful, yet dignified. Unself-conscious and yet somehow . . . silly."

"*You're* silly!" I said. "Mo-om? Dad's getting goofy again!"

Mrs. Van Gent's elbow was on the table, her hand covering her face. When she took it away I could see she was grinning. She looked at Dad.

"Wouldn't you just like to forget this romantic-dinner-for-two business and join us?"

Dad put his hand on his chest. "Who, me?" He

looked around like maybe she was talking to somebody else.

"Yes, all of you. We'd like it, really."

"Well, I hadn't thought about it, but I suppose we could. We've got plenty of food. Beth?"

"Why not?" Mom said from the kitchen. "Robby can have a hot dog instead of salmon."

"Sure, why not?" Then Dad leaned over to Mrs. Van Gent and added real confidentially, "It might surprise you to hear this, but formal's not really our style anyway."

"No!" Mrs. Van Gent said. Then she burst out laughing.

I knew she was laughing about last week. It was like the same thought—Dad in the shredded T-shirt—popped into everyone's head at the same time. We all looked at each other and cracked up.

Finally Mrs. Van Gent got herself under control. "What I'm really dying to know is"—and now her blue eyes twinkled—"what kind of games are we playing after dinner?"

Well, they didn't actually play games, but Mom and Dad sat around talking with Steve and "Heidi" long after dinner was over. From my loft I could hear them down below, stretches of talk and little bursts of laughter.

I like books with happy endings, don't you? But real life's never quite like that. It always keeps going on to the next thing—happy, sad, or whatever. But at least I'd reached the end of *this* bunch of worries. Nobody was going to take me away from my family. Nobody was going to take me away from Nekomah Creek.

For the first time in weeks, I felt safe. And tired, too, in a good sort of way. I wouldn't be able to read more than two chapters tonight. Not after all that running around on the soccer field.

I was already dozing, in fact, when I remembered: tomorrow was—ta da—Powell's Books! I lay there, my eyes drooping again, watching the fire's shadows flickering on the ceiling, thinking about that City of Books. How would I ever choose which ones to buy? And what a fun problem to have.

I looked forward to a long, wet winter. Lots of dark, rainy nights to sit by the wood stove and read.

Yup, I love books. But you know what? Real life's not bad either.

About the Author

LINDA CREW lives with her husband, Herb, and their children, Miles, Mary, and William, at Wake Robin Farm in Corvallis, Oregon. Her other books are *Children of the River* and *Someday I'll Laugh About This*. *Children of the River* won Honorable Mention in the Fifth Annual Delacorte Press Prize for an Outstanding First Young Adult Novel Contest. It also won the International Reading Association's Children's Book Award for 1990 in the Older Reader Category, was chosen as a Best Book for Young Adults by the American Library Association, and was the 1989 Honor Book for the Golden Kite Award given by the Society of Children's Book Writers.

About the Book

The illustrations by Charles Robinson are done in pen and ink and wash.

The text is set in 12 point Vermilion with Roman Shaded Elongated used for display. The book was designed by Lynn Braswell.